The Dance
of the
Mothers

OTHER BOOKS BY MILLICENT DILLON

FICTION

Baby Perpetua and Other Stories
The One in the Back Is Medea (novel)

NONFICTION

A Little Original Sin: The Life and Work of Jane Bowles
After Egypt: Isadora Duncan and Mary Cassatt
Out in the World: The Selected Letters of Jane Bowles
(editor)

The Dance of the Mothers

by
MILLICENT DILLON

[signature: Millicent Dillon]

A WILLIAM ABRAHAMS BOOK

DUTTON

DUTTON
Published by the Penguin Group
Penguin Books USA, Inc., 375 Hudson Street,
New York, New York 10014, U.S.A.
Penguin Books Ltd, 27 Wrights Lane,
London W8 5TZ, England
Penguin Books Australia Ltd, Ringwood,
Victoria, Australia
Penguin Books Canada Ltd, 2801 John Street,
Markham, Ontario, Canada L3R 1B4
Penguin Books (N.Z.) Ltd, 182–190 Wairau Road,
Auckland 10, New Zealand

Penguin Books Ltd, Registered Offices:
Harmondsworth, Middlesex, England

First published by Dutton, an imprint of New American Library,
a division of Penguin Books USA Inc.
Distributed in Canada by McClelland & Stewart Inc.

First Printing, June, 1991

10 9 8 7 6 5 4 3 2 1

Copyright © Millicent Dillon, 1991
All rights reserved

 REGISTERED TRADEMARK—MARCA REGISTRADA

Library of Congress Cataloging-in-Publication Data:
Dillon, Millicent.
    The dance of the mothers: a novel/by Millicent Dillon.
        p.   cm.
    "A William Abrahams book."
    ISBN 0-525-93312-3
    I. Title.
    PS3554.I43D36   1991
813'.54—dc20   90-24942
                                                                                    CIP

Printed in the United States of America
Set in Baskerville
Designed by Eve L. Kirch

PUBLISHER'S NOTE

This is a work of fiction. Names, characters, places, and incidents either are the products of the author's imagination or are used fictitiously, and any resemblance to actual persons, living or dead, events, or locales is entirely coincidental.

To John

1

Now that I am old and often still, I no longer believe what I once believed, that motion is the opposite of stillness. Then, I remember, I feared and hated stillness as if it were a kind of death. So how was it, I ask myself, that I had come to live a life that was like a confinement, a life that based its meaning on protection, on being protected, on holding on, on holding off?

Surrounded now by others who live lives in which moving has multiplied—till there is almost nothing to life but motion—in a world in which protection has come to seem an illusion, I am puzzled by what I chose. (For I did choose that life, though I may have preferred to think it was chosen for me.)

I am convinced that life must have been boring at times, perhaps often (though boredom is a poor word for the paralyzing entanglement of unclear and opposing impulses). I recall that it was isolated. (I may exaggerate that isolation.) I believe that it was numbing.

Yet even then I knew that beneath—or within—the boredom and the isolation and the numbing lurked something unclear, not to be paid attention to, not to be thought about, above all not to be told.

I knew, even then, especially then, the terrible danger in telling. I said to myself, It can be told later. Later. There is always time. I resolved, in the meantime, to keep silent. I assured myself it did not deserve attention, it did not deserve the full weight of thought. (Yes, the thought still persists that attention must be deserved.)

But to be old is to be almost out of time. It is to be incessantly made aware of small tremblings and sudden shifts, of new kinds of laboring in your body. To be old—especially to be an old woman—is to be passed by unseen, to be diminished, while at the same time you have grown large, pregnant with untold story.

I am only waiting to be delivered.

I look back through time as across space, to another room, a room like the one I am in, except it has a transparent wall. She, Anna, the young woman I once was, sits waiting.

I watch, I wait. I am audience. She is performer. She starts to move; she stops; she starts to move. When she moves, I move. When she stops, I stop.

In the midst of this alternation I feel a quickening in my nerves and muscles, I feel the beginning of an opening of my bones, a letting out, a letting go, a letting in, a multiplying. More than one—one other, two others—they also are starting, they also are stopping.

2

Earlier we had seen Ninta leap. We had seen her begin, we had seen her end, but she—it—the leap that possessed her had moved too fast to follow. It was a darting so perilous, so instantaneous, she seemed to have gone from one place to the other without being in the space between.

Now Ninta stood in place, earthbound, a woman of uncertain age—How can a dancer's age be guessed?— slender in her black leotard to the point of frailty. Her intense eyes were hooded above the high cheekbones. Her long red hair was pulled back severely.

Behind her was a small elevated stage with a sagging blue curtain that was always closed. At the opposite end of the parish hall was a choir loft, accessible by a flight of narrow stairs. Hanging from the high ceiling, lamps on long metal rods cast circles of interlocking brightness. Only if one looked directly up into the lights did they seem to glare. There were no windows in the hall.

Standing before us, she did a slow, sustained gesture with her arms. Then she had us repeat the motion over and over again. "No movement, not even the smallest, is to be done here without full attention to its purpose, its meaning, its sequence." She moved through the room slowly, observing each one, correcting. She stopped behind me. "The flow of the movement is being stopped here." She touched me on the right shoulder. "Try to let go, Anna."

Staring at the sagging blue curtain, I tried to let go, failed, tried again, then stopped. The more I tried to release the tension, the greater it became. I felt a band of tightness in the muscles at the back of my neck, rigidifying my shoulders, my upper back.

Beside me was Leona—Leona with the beautiful, serene face and ungainly body—her arms flopping awkwardly. She looked so foolish . . .

Directly in front of Leona, her back to me, was Aleida. In her slender body, with her long neck and sharply sloping shoulders, she was repeating Ninta's instructions exactly—yet not quite exactly. For all the correctness with which she moved, in her motion there was a hint of travesty.

3

We were at the kitchen table, finishing dinner. It was as it always was, Amy and I on one side of the gray Formica table, Rebecca and Gregg opposite. The table was supported on one end by a metal angle that was anchored in the concrete slab below the gray asphalt tile. The other end was bolted to the kitchen counter. Above the table a long black cabinet was cantilevered out from the counter wall, which divided the kitchen and the living room.

I had asked Gregg, as I always asked him—the end of the meal ritual—about his work, a leading question. He was answering (following? leading?). I sensed that Rebecca and Amy were about to grow restless. In a minute they would say they were done, would ask if they could leave the table. I was listening to Gregg. He was talking about a new kind of disk drive, about rotating drums and random access memory. He was racing ahead, caught up in the enthusiasm of ideas, of possibilities, caught up in the telling.

Amy and Rebecca were asking, I was telling them they could leave the table, reminding them to wash their hands. I was still listening, Gregg was still talking. Then suddenly, I had fallen behind. I heard him speaking, but I was not listening. At that moment I knew that I was going to betray him.

(With whom? For what?)

Shaken, I jumped up from the table. I went over to the sink. I stood there. I turned on the water, I started to rinse the dishes.

"I'm listening," I said, over the sound of the running water.

"What?" Gregg said.

"I'm listening," I said again. I tried to listen, tried to catch up. But he had left me far behind. I did not want to ask him to repeat what he had said. I heard the metal legs of the chair squeak on the tile as he got up. He was beside me now, placing his dishes on the counter. I opened the dishwasher. I pulled the upper wire shelf out. I began to load the glasses.

I turned off the water. "What was that you said to me yesterday, about those numbers, about the age of the youngest child and the oldest child—"

"Oh that—that if you have two children, when the oldest is as old as you were when the youngest was born, then the youngest will be as old as you were when the oldest was born. And you will be the sum of their ages."

"So—"

"So since you were twenty-six when Rebecca was born and twenty-nine when Amy was born, when Rebecca is twenty-nine, Amy will be twenty-six, and you will be fifty-five."

"Fifty-five—" He laughed. He put his hand upon my right shoulder. "It's a long way away," he said.

I felt myself let go—a little.

"I'll get their bath ready," he said.

I turned on the water again. Fifty-five. I was thinking of a woman older than fifty-five. I was remembering a play I had seen when I was eighteen. It was about a young woman, about to get married, excited, joyful, ready for the future, when suddenly some kind of an accident took place—a fall? Was it a fall? The woman's mind had been affected and she'd lost her sense of the present. She'd lived for years, immobilized, in a twilit world that no one—no reality—could penetrate. And then one day when she was very old, there was a second accident— another fall?—and she came back to the present. She thought she was as she had been, still that young woman of twenty or so. To her nothing had happened. But she was an old woman, her life nearly over. She looked back over a hole in time. Her body had lived in time but she had lost the years.

I had wept uncontrollably in that theater, lamenting as if I were the one who had lost a lifetime. But even as I wept, I hated the weeping, hated the feeling that I was being played upon so easily, too easily, my feelings being pushed this way and that under another's direction. And I was going along, consenting, more than consenting, welcoming the lamentation. Yet the story was false; it felt false. Everything was in terms of outer appearance, summed up, smoothed over, not serious somehow. Who really knew what the woman—if there was such a woman—had lived in her mind, what lives she had lived, maybe multiple lives, in that twilit sleep? Who had the right to say that passage of time was nothing for her, that it was a hole? All during that period her body had been changing; it had its own story to tell. And when she returned to everyday life, maybe it was still there, available somehow. Who was to say no?

I pulled out the lower wire basket of the dishwasher. I bent over and loaded the dishes into it. Even in memory—especially in memory—it was necessary to fight against manipulation, deception that swept you up and rolled you around with its intention to make you weep, make you regret, make you think things were irretrievably lost.

I felt the tightness, the stoniness in my upper back, in my neck, in my shoulders. I thought it might be some memory, some feeling I was resisting, something I had refused to pay attention to, that insisted on attention the only way it could, by seizing hold, by not letting go, by keeping me in its grasp, encapsulated, as if in armor.

4

"No," Ninta said sharply, "I am not interested in your expressing your feelings. I'm interested in movement, in your exploring changes in dynamics, in levels, in the use of space—"

"But—"

"That's one of the reasons I told you to read Ortega's book, *The Dehumanization of Art*. He says that all of us—whether we recognize it or not—are in a new universe, a new time, a new space. We can't rely on the old forms any more, even the old forms of feeling. For anybody interested in art—at even the most beginning level—it's necessary to go through a process of depersonalization or abstraction, to—Just a minute, let me finish. It is necessary to move in a way appropriate to this time, to this place, to this new universe that is being disclosed to us. And we're certainly not going to get to the appropriate forms and motions through self-indulgence, through what people call 'expressing yourself.' If you do that you'll just keep on going round and round in the same circles, always preoccupied with the self—one's personal history—and nothing else.

"To do what I'm talking about requires a stripping down—of self, of form, of everything—in order to be able to begin again. To really begin, to be open to the unexpected. To translate everything into motion—all hints, questions, urges, thoughts, doubts—whatever. For example," and here Ninta opened her arms in a sharp, stunning gesture. "How could this movement continue? Where would it take you, if you allowed yourself to follow its lead? It might move you forward," and here she broke into an erratic run, "and that motion might take you into this—" She slowed, swayed to the side and began to turn, spiraling down then up.

She stopped, she smiled. Even her smile was intense in her hawklike face. "You have to experience it in your own bodies. Each of you, start out with that first movement I gave you. Follow it out in your own way, without any preconceptions. Change the tempo to any tempo that suits you. Use the space as you need to."

I took my place upon the floor with the others. I stood without moving, trying to think of what one had to do to abstract oneself from feeling. Would one think of oneself as an object? Would one simply erase—things? I opened my arms as Ninta had done. What was I to do now? A spasm toward movement began in my mind, but I rejected it. Another came. I turned that down too. Whatever I thought of—for thought came first—seemed predirected, preconceived, false, not basic.

Up ahead of me was the closed blue curtain, ragged and unkempt. I turned around and faced the choir loft.

9

I saw that the others were all moving. Only I was still. I forced myself to begin, to make a gesture, any gesture. I must begin with what Ninta had given us. I started, I stopped. I felt corrupted, raw, vulgar, common . . .

"Let's finish up," Ninta called out.

"I'm not ready," someone said.

"You've done enough for the first time. Remember this is just a beginning exercise. Who would like to show us what they did?"

Leona—beautiful Leona—raised her hand and came forward awkwardly, a step or two behind her own intentions. "I don't know if this is what you wanted . . ." She opened her arms, then slowly, uneasily lowered herself to the ground. She opened out her arms further, as if she were carrying a large round weightless object, and began to lift it and herself, ending on her knees, her arms outstretched.

"That was very lovely," Ninta said. "It was simple and convincing."

Next it was Aleida's turn. Her improvisation was almost an exact repetition of the movement that Ninta had shown us. But in Aleida's body it was profoundly altered. There was a suggestiveness in her emphasis on the motion of the hips and pelvis. On her face, in her dark round eyes with their brilliant whites, was the excitement of being looked at by others, of being the center of attention.

"Very, very nice," Ninta said.

When my turn came, I stepped forward with a small dread. I made myself begin. I opened my arms. I stood there, unmoving. My left hand began to clutch. It stopped. It started. It stopped. It was like a stammering. In a panic I thought, I have nothing to show. Yet in the midst of paralysis I noticed a twinge in myself, an ache, a grievance (against what had led me into this ridiculous position, into too easily agreeing to do what was asked of me) that led me bit by bit to follow after, to bend over into a crouch, until my head hung forward, my arms entwined across my belly. But it—I—did not stop there. My right hand, still following, began to pull me out of that crouch, reached up toward the peaked ceiling, toward the glare of the lights, reaching and straining, till a sharp jerking motion of my shoulder pulled me down back again into the crouch, clutching my belly—

I heard someone laugh. Was it Aleida? It sounded like Aleida. I looked at her. She was half-turned away, facing the stage.

"That is interesting, Anna," said Ninta, "but the energy seems muddied so the movement is not clear. It feels as if you're forcing it. Try letting go into it more."

"How do I do that?" I asked, masking resentment. (Yes, Leona's movement was "lovely." Yes, Aleida's was "very, very nice." But mine was "muddied.")

"You have to try and clarify it. Simplify it."

"But—"

"You have to be patient. Just wait for the right impulse to appear. You'll know it when it comes."

I am tired of being patient, the thought came.

5

In the middle of the night, unable to sleep, I turned on the light. Gregg continued to sleep, deeply. Light did not bother him—it never did. Whereas, no matter how deep my sleep, if a light went on, a signal came to my brain, Get up, get up. I could not refuse it. I was at the mercy of light, as well as too many other things.

I got up and walked down the hallway. At the open door of the children's room, I listened. I heard a stirring. I turned on the light. They were like Gregg, they would not waken. I covered Rebecca, who had thrown her covers off. From the doorway I looked at them again. Each sleeping so soundly, each even in sleep making a characteristic gesture: Rebecca sprawled on her back, arms out; Amy, on her stomach, cuddling, nestling under the blankets. I turned off the light.

In the kitchen I took a small stainless saucepan from the cupboard below the built-in range. It was my habit to drink a cup of warm milk when I could not sleep. As I placed the saucepan on the burner, feeling the smooth Bakelite handle in my palm, I felt a tightening, a clotting like the onset of rage, the impulse to hurl the pan across

12

the room. How it—the pan—like other things waited so stolidly in stillness, offering itself up for use. Guardian of habit, reinforcing and sustaining the given.

Yet how could one be angry at a thing—at things? In themselves, through themselves, they offered protection. They were guarantors of the evenness of life. So, if one was not a fool, one had to take care of them, maintain them, allow them their necessary continuity. It was a pact of sorts, an exchange, care as guarantee for care, a pact that one broke at one's own risk.

From the refrigerator I got a bottle of milk and estimated a cupful as I poured it out into the pan. I put the bottle back in the refrigerator. In the light of the small bulb I was struck by what a mess it was. No, I had not taken proper care. Things were shoved in, jammed in too tightly, old things at the back that should have been thrown out—but weren't—not leaving room for new things. I'll clean it tomorrow, I told myself and shut the door.

I went into the living room. I turned on the light. I sat on the black and white couch in darkness. Across from me was the wall of floor to ceiling windows, uncurtained, facing the patio and backyard, away from the street. The deep garden was screened from the empty lot behind by a newly planted hedge of rhamnus and feijoa. Suddenly, sitting there, I had the sense that someone was just outside, on the patio, looking in. I strained to see in the darkness. Clearly there was no one there. Yet the feeling persisted that a woman, an older woman, an old woman was watching me across the years as through glass, waiting for me to move, ready to make out of my moving the stuff of her memory.

6

Lately it has come to Aleida that the life she has is not the life she was meant to have. She has read or heard of others who are adventurous, who never doubted their willingness to risk, who went to New York to live in a cold-water flat, who led a Bohemian life, playing, drinking, loving, creating.

Performing, her life should have been performing. But performing what, she is not sure.

Aleida realizes that she has only an approximate sense of herself.

* * *

For a long time Aleida has managed her existence in terms of the conviction that she is needy, has to be comforted and protected. The thought that Ken is there, beside her, is what has given her stability—even in the night, in dreams. But since coming to Peralta early this year, she has begun to doubt her own assumption. She now judges that what seems to be neediness in her is nothing but a response to Ken's need to be needed. For which she, immediately, feels a small but certain revulsion toward him.

*   *   *

Aleida had a dance memory. It was hard, sharp, corrosive at the core, though uncertain in detail. When she recalled it, as she did frequently now that she was taking Ninta's class, it was with a strenuous attack. (Remembering, for Aleida, was a little like forcing a sense of herself out of the haze of history.)

She is hurrying through the aisle of the department store. She is eight, perhaps nine. On either side of her are display cases with things for sale. Her head barely reaches the top of the counter, but she is tall enough to see the many things that can be bought.

Beside her, behind her, all around her, is her mother—propelling her. Rose is large, with a large bosom and dark eyes and thick dark hair. (She is not, as she will someday become, frail, withered, with sagging breasts, bony, light, so light, almost transparent.) Aleida runs in front of her, her representative to the outside world, running through the aisle of the department store, about to rise up on the escalator to where she will take part in the tryouts.

Rose has told Aleida why the musical is being sponsored by the department store. She does not believe in withholding anything from Aleida, just because she is a child. And besides, Rose is an explainer. The government has the NRA and relief and the WPA—and the store has this musical for children, with children. Later, when times are better, the customers will remember how generous the store was and will come back and buy. And in the meantime—she opens her arms wide, palms up—"We're ready."

They ride up the escalator to the top floor, as if they are ascending to an ideal future. They get off, they see boxes and boxes, storerooms, they see a sign saying "Tryouts." In a large windowless room a man is playing a tune on an upright piano. There is no one else in the room. Rose rushes over to him. "Is the tryout over? Are we too late?" Aleida can hear the fear in her voice. Is it possible that one can be robbed of success because a clock stopped at home? Is that how chancy the world is, and unfair? But no, her mother is told by the man at the piano—he has a smooth pink face and smooth white hair—the children's tryouts are not until three. And it's only two-thirty.

Aleida and her mother sit on straight chairs against the wall. There is nothing to do but wait. Here Aleida is, ready to move, ready to win, and time itself is still. No way to make it go faster. She swings her legs back and forth from the knee, she kicks them against the rungs of the chair. Is it time yet? she asks her mother. Her mother shrugs her heavy shoulders. Stop kicking the chair, she says. Aleida tries to listen to the music the man is playing. She can't listen. She gets off the chair. Sit down, her mother says. I'm thirsty, she says. You'll have to wait, her mother says. There's no water here.

Soon other girls come in with their mothers. They sit on chairs around the edges of the room, mothers and daughters together. Impatiently, Rose gets up. She gets Aleida up. They stand, waiting for the moment to be called. Rose taps her foot, her ankle surprisingly slim in her high-heeled shoes, her foot moving in time to the tune the smooth man is playing. Yet Aleida knows she is watching, waiting to spring forward, to propel Aleida forward.

The call comes, the other mothers rise, the other girls jump up. But Aleida is at the front of the line already.

"Let's see you do the time step. Let's see you do a

backbend." Aleida is giddy at the thought of others watching her. She does not have to look to see that in the audience of mothers her mother is nodding, Good, Good, Good.

Out of all the girls in the room, ten are chosen; Aleida is one of the ten. The unchosen have to leave. The remaining daughters smile, the mothers smile, except for one girl with blond curls who clings to her mother and weeps that she wants to go home. Don't be a crybaby, her mother says, tight-lipped.

The smooth-haired man calls on the girls to come forward once again. He gives them a series of easy steps to do. Then he gives them a more difficult one, a turn with a fast break. Aleida picks up the step faster than the others. She feels that she is shining, that she is pulling other people's eyes to her, that they can't help watching her.

You, says the smooth man, pointing to Aleida, step out front. You'll be the leader.

Riding down the escalator, Aleida tells herself that it was already in the sound of her name. Aleida, leader. She was meant to be out in front of the others. She was meant to have a costume more beautiful than theirs. Below her, around her, Aleida sees all the things that she'll buy some day, for herself and for her mother. She can see it now, the buying, the giving. Descending, Aleida hears a sound like applause in the air.

*   *   *

Hours, days pass in practicing. It is necessary to repeat and repeat the steps of the dance. Long before the others have it right, Aleida knows all the steps and the timing perfectly. She has her costume now. More beautiful than all the other costumes, it makes her stand out even before she begins.

Sharply now, the smooth man approaches. They are rehearsing on the big stage where they will do the performance. Aleida is sure he is going to say, Good, Good, to her. She can see her mother nodding, Yes, Yes, her darkness nodding in the auditorium. But the smooth man does not say, Good, Good. He says, You're going to have to get back in the line. Then he puts a slob of a girl, a fat blond girl, in front, a girl who never even tried out with the others. Aleida has to give her her beautiful costume. It'll never fit her, Aleida sees, but that does not stop her heart from sinking like a stone.

They do the dance again with the fat slob in front, tripping over her feet. As soon as the rehearsal is over, her mother rushes up to her.

"What happened?"

"I don't know."

"You were doing it right, weren't you?"

"Yes, I was doing it right."

"So why, I'm going to ask why."

"No, don't."

"You think I'll let them get away with this."

Aleida watches her, squirming for her, for herself, seeing the fierceness mount in her mother's face as she goes over to the smooth man, insisting on his attention at once. Yes, Aleida wants it all to be made right, the way it was before, the way it was supposed to be, herself at the front of the line. But something in her, hard and dark, new grown, tells her that it will not be so. Aleida sees the man turn his back, she sees her mother walk away, her shoulders turned inward, shabbily. She sees something else, in her mother's face, something she has never seen before: the fear of losing in the face of someone who has already lost almost everything.

*   *   *

At home in the small dark flat, her mother says bitterly, "He wouldn't give me a reason. But there's a reason. You can see she's got no talent, she can't move. She's nowhere near as good as you are. So why did he do it? Why did he take you out of the front spot and put her in? I'll tell you why. I bet I know why. The girl's a relative, his relative or the relative of the one who owns the store, one or the other. I don't need to be told."

"I don't want to go back," Aleida says.

"Don't whine."

"I'm not whining."

"It's better to have something than nothing. Even in the line you'll be better than her, better than any of the others. Go back and show them. We're not quitters in this family."

Once more her mother tried to beguile her with promises: what will be, how it will all be made up for, all that has happened. Don't let yourself be upset by a man like that. People like him, they come and go. We're the stayers. What matters is that you believe in yourself, in your future.

Aleida pretended to listen, she pretended to agree, but she was not persuaded. She will not get me back into that again, so that we both end up the same, both still hoping, both beaten, she told herself. She knew now how dangerous her mother was, how she could lead you into believing in what (and in whom) you should never have believed in the first place. The best way was to shut off the wanting (and the believing), not let it really get hold of you. You could pretend you believed, if you had to, but at least all the time you knew you really didn't. Only then could you be safe—behind your own eyes.

7

But now, in Peralta, Aleida's wanting could no longer be contained. It was slipping out, leaking out, growing without limit, nourished by the soft gentle air, by the benign sun, by the peacefulness of the country-side, by the absence of harsh seasons and danger.

Aleida wanted—she didn't know what she wanted. (She wanted to make up for lost time.) She wanted success, fame, she wanted money, things. She wanted what others had. It was as though everything she saw that belonged to someone else was wrapped up, labeled for her eyes only, "Not mine." So just to look, just to see what others had, how well they were doing, sent her into a rage. But the rage itself had an even greater wanting of its own. It swallowed you up, used you up, till there was nothing of you left but itself. You had to waylay it, limit it, pretend it was going to go away, or you'd go nuts. You couldn't let go into the absolute belief that there was some power in the world that let others have—unjustly—but that con-demned you—just as unjustly—to not having.

And it wasn't as though only a person here and a per-son there had these things. It was everybody in Peralta: men, women, and children, who had what she didn't have, who had what she hadn't had, who had what she—possibly—might never have. It was even worse than when she was a kid. Then, during the Depression everybody was having a hard time. But now everybody was doing better, everybody was starting all over again, living in a new house, with new furniture and a new car. Everybody but her and Ken, that is. With him it was: Not yet, Maybe later, I'll see.

Later. Always later.

Look at their furniture, just look at it. A secondhand couch from the Goodwill, with a hole in the upholstery, and a blanket over it so the hole wouldn't show; an old Morris chair with the leather pillows scratched and peeling; an outdoor redwood table and benches for a dining room set. You couldn't even call it furniture. It was stuff, temporary stuff.

And their car? A 1948 Studebaker, in and out of the shop all the time but they had to keep it because he liked its "futuristic" lines.

And this house? Not for him a new house in a new tract. That was too ordinary. No, he had to have a cheap old cottage in the old part of town. And it wasn't even their house. They were renting, not buying.

"Why don't we get one of those new tract houses?" She said it right out, boldly. "You can get it with practically no down payment at all with your G.I. Bill."

"What's wrong with this place?"

"Why pay rent instead of owning? All that money just goes down the drain. It's just as cheap to buy."

He shrugged.

"Besides, everything's falling apart here, the roof and the plumbing, and the fence—"

"I'll get around to fixing those things."

"When?"

"Take it easy, will you?"

She held herself back for a moment, but then she couldn't stop herself any longer. "This place is—ugly."

"It's not ugly. It's practical, basic, down to earth. It doesn't have any pretensions. It has character." He laughed his charming laugh.

She too laughed, but harshly. "You call leaking plumbing character? Sometimes," and now she had to go further, faster, "I think you're afraid of the thought of having anything nice." She realized, even as she was saying it, that she was pushing him over that edge where easy charm suddenly gave way, and he fell into a strangeness where she could no longer pursue him, some dense thickness inside his own skin. But she had to keep on, it was like picking away at a scab. "Sometimes I think you need misery, that you want misery, that you're not satisfied unless you—"

"Get off my back," he said. It wasn't nice, it wasn't charming. She saw the softness thicken about him.

She retreated, she knew she had to retreat. "I was just thinking about it as an investment."

"An investment? Since when are you thinking about investments?"

"Why shouldn't I?" She smiled and tossed her head.

He laughed, charmingly enough. How she had been seduced by that charm from the moment she had met him. All that it said about wanting and not wanting. About getting and not getting. She had been a prisoner of that charm, part of her still was, but she was beginning to see it for what it was. Here in Peralta, where there was a new light on everything, that charm was beginning to look like seediness, yes seediness, and she tied to him, was bound to be a loser who clung to losing like it was a lifeline.

* * *

When she first came into Ninta's class in the old parish hall, she swallowed hard, as if there was still the residue of the dance memory in her throat, in her mouth. Around her she saw others' bodies, some taller, some shorter, some fatter, some slimmer.

She put herself at the front of the class. She kept her eyes on Ninta, she didn't look away. She followed every motion Ninta made. She discovered she still had the capacity for picking up things instantaneously—gestures, patterns, steps. Her sense of rhythm was still perfect. She still had that instinctive orientation in space, to moving in space, so she never got turned around. They were talents that had been sitting inside her, unused, waiting patiently for their turn, ready to make up for their lost time.

After the first class Ninta told her she had a real talent for dance. After several more sessions she told her she was doing so well she'd like to work individually with her, she'd like to train her to be her assistant. Of course Aleida said she'd be very grateful to be her assistant, which she would be, for a while. She'd pick Ninta's brain—and body. She'd have to put up with more talk, more theories, all that shit about abstraction and old feelings that weren't felt anymore, and new feelings that you were going to somehow magically find, like under a stone.

How could anybody be so disconnected from the real world? Why didn't she perform? If Aleida danced the way Ninta danced, she'd be performing all the time. But Ninta was a loser too. You could tell, just by looking at her face, at the sharp hawklike nose with its nostrils that seemed to have smelled tragedy once and still was sniffing it out.

Looking at the closed blue curtain, Aleida thought, What would it be like to be up before an audience, right at the front of the stage, receiving wave after wave of applause, bowing, and taking it all in, and getting even more with every bow? Wait, wait, it will come. If I can just wait something will come. Will it come? Will I know the right moment to leap, to jump? She had thrown away so many opportunities in the past, by refusing to be part of anything, by pretending she didn't care. She had thrown away the baby with the bath water.

Baby, I have no baby. I'm not sorry. Why should I want to bring someone else into this world with all their wanting that would have to be satisfied? What would be left for me? If I don't get it myself, who will?

She shivered, feeling how fear was braided irrevocably into wanting. I'll have to be careful, I won't forget what has happened in the past, how it is when you're going along on top, queen of the mountain, king of the mountain, the mountain itself, and suddenly it all dissolves into shit, you are covered with shit, you've fallen into shit. That's what the mountain always was.

"No, I am not interested in your expressing your feelings ..." Ninta was off and running on her theories again, insisting on their doing that stupid improvisation. How Aleida hated improvisation. But she'd done it, she'd made herself do it, giving Ninta back just what she'd given them, a mirror image.

Then Anna had done that movement, with that crouching and crazy jerking. Aleida had laughed, she couldn't help it. It wasn't that it was funny, not funny ha-ha-ha. In fact, it wasn't funny at all. There was something ugly and sickening about that movement. Naked. Not covered over. Aleida shivered at the thought of such exposure. To show such a thing in front of others was asking to be laughed at. That's not what I want. I want ... I want ... I want the ones watching to wish they were me.

But for now she had to wait, she had to be cautious. She couldn't even plan her next move. She had to wait, see what came, then capitalize—yes, capitalize, on that. And in the meantime she had to watch out, to defend herself, to see that no one took her place.

Turning to look at the stage again, she felt as if her edge—her outline itself—was becoming sharper.

8

Into the town of Peralta, totally unexpectedly, Ralph Herbert came, offering new possibilities, a new beginning, a renaissance of all the arts and especially of the art of performance. He issued a call for any and all residents to come and join him, to attend the first meeting, the first tryouts, for the first performance of his first production at the Community Theater.

Ninta warned us. Clearly he was a con man, a windbag, a humbug. She had read that interview in the local paper with his pretentious invitation: "I want everybody to feel free to come and work with me. Whatever anybody has ever wanted to do in performance that they've felt shy or embarrassed about, because they thought they weren't good enough, or good-looking enough, or talented enough, now is their chance. We are all artists, each one as good as the next, no one better than the other."

"Oh, he makes it sound so easy: 'Just come and perform,'" Ninta said. "You know me well enough to know that I'm not opposed to the idea that everybody, at some level, is creative. Of course that's true. But that's not the point." She became more and more agitated. She began to pace up and down before the students. She stopped, she went on. "But this is performance that he's talking about. Do you know what is involved in true performance? I don't only mean the years and years of preparation. I mean the impulse behind it. Do you think the impulse is fun? Do you think the impulse is self-congratulation? Do you think performance is just getting up on the stage to be seen, to be applauded? What he doesn't tell you about is the risk."

We listened but we were not persuaded. What risk could she possibly mean? Was she just jealous? We saw she saw she had not convinced us. Her eyes glinted with sorrow or pain. Her nose became sharper.

Suddenly she shrugged, she turned away, then turned back. "Of course, if you want to go, it's up to you. It's not my place to stop you."

* * *

On the bare stage of the Peralta Community Theater we waited. Some of us stretched, a few talked, most were silent, furtively looking about, warily judging each other's bodies. From the wings appeared Ralph Herbert, a paunchy man with fleshy jowls and thinning hair. Wearing a shiny blue suit, he looked like what he was, an aging actor whose looks had gone to seed. He cleared his throat. He put his hand in his pocket. He pulled out several torn pieces of paper. One dropped upon the floor. He leaned over to pick it up. He farted loudly. Someone laughed nervously. He stood up, he reached into his pocket for his glasses, he put them on. He took them off again. He cleared his throat.

"If you think about it—" he began, then paused meaningfully, "If you think about it, you will realize that in life we—each one of us in our own way—makes a gift of our creative power to others every single day. And here," he swept his right arm in an arc to indicate the stage, "here we will just continue to do what we do in life." He paused again. "Here we will give of ourselves, of our creative power, not out of the desire for money— obviously no one will get paid here—but out of devotion. Yes, this is the amateur theater and we are all amateurs. But what does that mean? *Amo—amas—amat—amare—* means to love. To be an amateur means to love the thing for itself, to love the theater for itself."

He looked out into the auditorium. He dropped his head. He stood in apparently somber thought. He raised his head and smiled. "Have I made myself clear?"

Yes, we nodded, Yes.

"Good," he said. "Good." His voice became more intimate, affable. "Friends, and I hope we will soon be friends, who of you can tell me, What is a play? Anyone? No one?" He waited. "What is a play but a sequence of actions presented on a stage in performance before an audience? And what is an audience but a group, a number of individuals, watching, listening, making up one body, as it were, a body in which all the individual parts have given up their own sense of self-consciousness to become part of the self-consciousness of the whole."

Again he stopped. He smiled. "Two profound human needs are bound up in the theater—amateur or not amateur—it doesn't matter. One is the need to perform before others, the need to be seen by others. The other, equally important, is the need to be part of a group, part of a spectacle, part of a ritual—part of an audience seeing."

Out of his jacket pocket he drew a frayed little book, which he held up. "I have here in my hand an invaluable little book. Let me tell you how I came upon it. I was walking one day, some years ago, in the city, ruminating, hardly conscious of my surroundings when suddenly before me on the sidewalk—right there on the sidewalk in front of me, I saw this book. It was lying face—that is, title down—next to a garbage can. Clearly someone had intended to discard it forever. I bent down, I picked it up, I put it in my pocket. I forgot about it until the next day when I once again put on my jacket. I began to leaf through it idly. But in one instant I knew there was nothing idle about this book and its effect upon me. That moment of stooping down, that moment of picking up that discarded book was—as it turned out—to be one of the guiding moments of my life. Often I say to myself, What if I hadn't been walking down that street, what if I had not stooped down, what then? What would my life have been?" He paused. He lowered the arm holding the book. "Odd, isn't it—or isn't it odd—how Fate puts things in our path? Often we rush through life, looking for the thing we think we should have, when right there before us—right in our path—is what we need. We have to learn to accept, learn to be shameless in accepting what is given to us, no matter how and when it is given. People talk about contrived plots in the theater. I tell you, there are no contrived plots in life."

"What is the plot of this production?" I asked impatiently.

"I'll get around to that in due time. As I was about to say, about audience—" He opened the book and started to read aloud. " 'The members of an audience give up their differences in intellect, their differences in character, and even their differences in history, to become united by the innate basic passions of the race. They revert to primal simplicity, to primal sensitiveness of the mind.' "

He lowered the book, leaned forward, and peered intently at the dancers. "And what are the things that this audience with their primal simplicity wants to see, wants to feel? Anyone? No one? They want to see a struggle, they want to take sides, they want to love, they want to hate, they want to believe, they want to be overcome by feeling and by sensation. Frankly, they don't give a damn about theories, about ideas. If you're going to take anything away from my little talk tonight, it should be this: Beware of theory, beware of abstraction in the theater. If you think about it, you will realize that the intellect is basically anti-theatrical. Anti-theatrical," he repeated. "What is it that the audience cares about? They care about love. Right? And," he held up his fingers and ticked off one by one, "anger, jealousy, revenge, ambition, lust, treachery, sacrifice.

"Take Shakespeare. He didn't have any new ideas, did he? He wasn't even progressive. He was a business man. But—" and here he leaned forward again, "he knew about people, he knew what they wanted." He stood for a moment with his head bowed, then raised it suddenly. "Are there any questions?"

"You said you were going to say something about plot."

"Plot, ah yes, plot." He shook himself as if he were shaking off water. "Actually, I don't look at plot as something that exists on its own. I see it as arising out of all the other elements of our work. Plot following, not leading. Do you get the picture? Any other questions? No? If not, I would like to introduce our dance adviser and choreographer, who, I'm sure, needs no introduction to you."

Aleida, who had been standing in the wings, came out on stage and stood beside Ralph. He beamed at her and put his arm familiarly around her shoulder. "I am happy to have Aleida as part of our team, giving us the benefit of her years of experience in the dance."

"I'm delighted to be able to help out," said Aleida, arching her long neck.

"That's the spirit, that's the kind of thing I like to hear. That's the kind of attitude that's going to make our New Theater one of the best, if not the best, on the coast." He gave her a little pat on the cheek.

"But now, you'll have to excuse me for a few minutes. I'm afraid I must leave you to make a short speech of welcome to the actors in the greenroom. But I will be back shortly. In the meantime, Aleida, will you get them warmed up?" He jumped off the stage, surprisingly deftly, for such a paunchy man.

9

So, as it turned out, Aleida had not had to wait very long to make her move. She had gone to see Ralph, she had cozied up to him, flattered him, and he had accepted her, swallowing everything she'd said about her experience here in the theater and there in the theater. (She'd borrowed liberally from what Ninta had told her about herself.) Aleida had known that he wouldn't check. He wasn't the checking kind, he was too busy with his little book, with his "primordial emotions," with his "importance of 'Identification' in the theater," one minute ranting about the intellect and the next going on about his "New 'natural' Theater."

Who did he think he was, Cecil B. DeMille? the new Messiah? What he actually was was a pompous ass, but what did it matter? What did matter was that with him, through him, she had been and would be able to make her move.

Here they were before her, the dancers, waiting for her instructions. She called them to attention. She felt the slightest tremor of fear. But then words remembered from Ninta's class came to her rescue, Ninta's way of beginning, her bends, her stretches, her swings and releases, her contractions, her extensions. Hearing herself say the words, her voice give the instructions, she felt herself grow surer. She was the one directing them, telling them what to do, stopping them if she wanted, starting them off again, changing anything she wanted to, selecting what suited her, no one else. Now she was the one on judgment's side.

*   *   *

After the bends, after the stretches, after the swings and releases—the women dutifully responding to her orders—Aleida had no more doubts. She was doing what she was meant to do, propelling with ease and power, getting them to move. She had them walk at random, changing directions at her command. "Walk forward, pick any direction. Now stop," she called out. "Turn, choose another direction. Walk. Stop," she called out again, and they stopped. "I don't want to see any muddying in your directions. I want to see which way you're going and how you're going to get there."

The women walked and stopped, turned and walked again. Some were hesitant, some overeager, some were too fast and some were too slow. There was Anna, energetically starting, stopping, starting, stopping, always a little too early, anticipating when she should have been waiting. And there came Leona, pitiful Leona, too heavy, bulging out of her leotard, confused even in a simple movement like this.

10

"Ready?" Ralph called out from the back of the auditorium.

"Ready," said Aleida.

He jumped up on the stage lightly. "Remind me, what were we going to do first? Ah yes, the solo. We're going to choose the one for the solo dance. Actually there are two solos but Aleida's going to do the first one, so it's only the second one we have to worry about."

Ralph gazed off into the distance; he seemed to be absorbed in reflection. Finally he spoke in a deep, ruminative voice. " 'The Dance of the Mother.' Whichever one of you is chosen to do this dance is going to have to communicate to the audience the feeling of this character. It doesn't matter that you haven't had the same experience as this woman has. You'll still know what that feeling is. I'm talking about basic primordial human feelings here, the ones we all share, those feelings that have existed throughout time—in human beings, in human nature. Human beings don't really change, no matter how we think we progress with our newer and faster machines. Certain things always stay the same: love and hate, birth and death, joy and grief, suffering, loss. The real plot of life never changes. If you think about it you will see that it's all very ..." he hesitated and put his hand to his brow.

Aleida stepped forward and started to say something but he held up his hand and stopped her. "... simple," he said.

He ran his hand over his thinning hair. "So now. That's your theme: Love. Care. Loss. Grief. I have a few ideas for movement to serve as guide for you."

He closed his eyes. Standing in silence on the stage in his shiny blue suit he looked seedy, faded. But suddenly—and it was impossible to detect the exact moment of transition—a change began in him. Something in him began to crumple, though he stayed upright. By the slightest tilt of the head, by the smallest drop of the shoulder, by an almost imperceptible shadowing of his face, he conveyed the sense of someone punctured, giving way. His hands fumbled, as if he were trying to ward off a blow. He seemed to fall into himself, into vacuity. He became moundlike and inert. His head turned from side to side. He saw but he did not see. His mouth opened, his lips moved but no sound came out. His hands pawed at the air, till it seemed there was no limit to his falling. Then suddenly, as if he were pulling a shroud around himself, came that gesture of shaking off—water or darkness—

"Okay, you got the picture? I'll tell you what. I'm going to sit at the back of the auditorium and you girls can move across the stage, down the diagonal, one at a time. And when you move, I want you to make me feel what you're feeling. Grief. Loss. Remember who you are, you're the grieving mother. I want to be able to see that feeling in your body, I want to feel that feeling, I want to identify with you."

At Aleida's orders the women came down the diagonal to the front of the stage, improvising. One followed upon the other, this one with her arms akimbo, head bent, that one stumbling and pulling at her hair, the next one skulking, animallike.

"Move more," Aleida shouted. "You're not moving enough, make it larger."

"Come on, Miss-Whatever-Your-Name-Is," Ralph's voice boomed. "Grief doesn't look like that. You have to open yourself up, let grief in, let it overwhelm you. Surrender to it like it was a lover."

Once again the women came down the diagonal. "No, no, no, no!" Ralph exploded. "What is going on here? Why is this so hard for you? Don't push so hard, let it slip up on you. Once, I remember, I was driving and there ahead of me, out in the road, was a thing—it had been a dog. I could just tell as I was passing it—or maybe I knew it even before—it was a dog, it had been a big dog. But all you could see going past was something like fur—something gray, and red, all red mixed up in it. I tell you, there was something about that that got to me. I had to pull over to the side of the road. I couldn't keep on going. I just sat there and cried like a baby. Maybe you've got something like that, that came on you unexpectedly, that you can show us in movement. In movement," he repeated, "not in your head."

"Okay," Aleida said sharply, "let's try it again. One by one."

Once more they came on the diagonal. One trembled, one cowered, one stumbled, one twisted in an ever-diminishing circle. Here came Anna with that same movement she had done in Ninta's class, that bending over into the crouch, the grasping, the twisting with one arm, the reaching out, the sudden sharp movement, back, down, in . . .

Why that again? What does that have to do with what we're doing? Aleida turned away in disgust.

And here came Leona, moving so slowly, as if she were dragging herself through mud, that fat slob. Not grief, thought Aleida, not grief.

11

Leona had no dance memory, had never even thought of herself as someone who could dance. She kidded about her awkwardness, said she had two left feet, in fact could not tell her right from her left. (When she was a child she had figured out how to tell which was her right hand. She would say the Pledge of Allegiance to herself and whatever hand would come up to her chest, that was the right one.) As for her sense of rhythm, sometimes she was on the beat, sometimes she wasn't. She couldn't tell when she was on any more than when she was off. Yet for all that, here she was having been chosen for a solo part.

It did not occur to Leona to question how or why this had come about. She was not in the habit of challenging what was. She had been told as a child—and she believed it—that one accepted what was given. She didn't think of accepting as enduring, since that implies hardness. Rather, she had the sense that, if there were hardness, she would be sheltered from it by others. When she was a child, and up to the time she left home, her mother had protected her. And then there was marriage and Norman.

When she had met him, the very first thing he had said to her was, "I want to marry you. I want to take care of you." She had smiled at the force and spontaneity of his intention. She took it into herself, welcomed it, cherished it, fell in love with it.

Placidity is not ordinarily thought of as passionate, but Leona passionately desired placidity. She wanted one thing to follow another in a predictable course. She felt as if random impulse had no place in her nature. She knew she was not a self-starter but that did not concern her. She admired others who, like Norman, were so purposeful and determined and always moving, getting new things started with a kind of fiery intensity. She was content to bask in that reflected glow.

But she had no desire to be like him. When he talked about his "fields," some kind of mathematical fields that had no relation to any actual fields on earth, she would listen uncomprehendingly and smile. She accepted his intensity with its nervous energy that at times went faster and faster, out of control, as if ideas were streaming into his head, into his nerves, he couldn't stop them. She was glad to offer him refuge from all that made him frantic, when he needed it, in her own placidity. It was, after all, an exchange: care for release, release for care.

* * *

But why, now that they had come to Peralta, was their bargain becoming unglued? He took refuge—in her—more and more frequently but he was still not appeased. In his restlessness he suddenly began to berate her for those qualities he had once so prized in her. She accepted that it was not at all unusual for marriages to reverse themselves momentarily but he kept pushing at her.

"You can't hang around the house doing nothing all the time," he said.

"Nothing?" she said and laughed. "I take care of the children."

"As far as I can see," he said, "they take care of themselves."

"Well," she said, "they are older now and they like to make their own decisions, do what they want to do."

"What do *you* want to do?" he asked her harshly.

"Me? I want to do what I'm doing."

"How can you not be bored?" he said. "How can you stand it, being in one place all the time? You're like an old stick in the mud."

"I don't feel like a stick in the mud," she said placidly.

"What's the use of talking?" he said.

What was the use of talking? He wouldn't believe her if she said what she felt. Getting out, wanting to move from place to place, was not natural to her. Sometimes she had the weird idea or rather she knew that he would think it was weird that she was like a plant—a plant, not a stick—rooted in the earth—not mud—with its tendrils waving in the soft air, opening and closing, opening and closing.

* * *

She soon began to see that the problem was that Norman was going against his nature, trying to be, to do, what he was not meant to be or do. When Gregg was promoted to project head, Norman had a fit. Why wasn't I made project head? he exploded. He would have been a terrible project head, why didn't he see that? He couldn't keep his mind on anything practical like budgets for two minutes. His mind was always jumping to an idea, two ideas, ten ideas, all coming together, till he was like a volcano erupting. Then he'd need someone like Gregg to calm him down. Many nights Gregg had come to the house and she'd heard them talking. Is this what you mean? Gregg would keep asking. Then Norman would stumble and start again, trying to make himself clear. But he didn't remember that now. All that he remembered was that he wanted to be project head and they didn't make him one. He was getting angrier day by day, the anger not making sense with his (still) boyish looks. Maybe that was another reason they didn't want to promote him, he didn't look old enough to be a manager, though he was almost forty.

She tried to soothe him. "But they did give you a good raise in May and your name is going to be on the patent for the new machine, you said so yourself—"

"What do you know about it? Have you been out working your butt off every goddam day without any recognition? Do you know what life is like out there, what it's really like? How could you possibly know, lounging around the house? Look at this mess," he went on in a fury, pointing to the white couch, full of cat hairs.

"I'll clean it," she said and went to the hall closet and got out the vacuum cleaner. When she came back into the living room, he was slumped in a chair, his head in his hands. She put down the hose. She went over to him and put her arms around him. "You're going to make yourself sick if you're not careful."

"I'm not going to be sick. Why is it, Leona, anytime there's an argument you have to rush and do something to cover it up? Why don't you argue more? Why do you have to keep giving in?"

"I don't like to argue. Arguing is—"

"What?"

She shivered. "It—"

"It's just talking."

"It's not just talking," she said stubbornly.

Then it was as it always was with them. In her flesh, in her softness, she offered him peace from what tormented him. In their lovemaking she was not seeking the inner pinpoint that leads to the final explosion. She felt capable of infinite absorption, as long as the surface of life was calm. It was in his pleasure, his release that became indistinguishable from her pleasure, that she found fulfillment without sharp ending.

*　*　*

When she saw the notice on the Co-op bulletin board about Ninta's dance class, she called and enrolled. She attended the classes faithfully. To her surprise she quite liked some of the exercises. Not the leaping, of course, which she always transformed into a hop, one foot taking one choice and one another because decision was forced on her when she wasn't ready for decision, so it never came out right. But the slow movements, particularly those in place, those she liked a lot. Nor did she care for Ninta's theories. They were really not natural, not necessary. But at least Norman was pleased that she was getting out. In fact he acted as if he was the one who was moving more. She thought of saying that to him but she didn't. Why irritate him when he was calmer? It was like so many other things in life. You must let them be.

So she kept going to Ninta's class. She had even gone

to the Community Theater to try out. And now she had been chosen by Ralph for the solo part.

*   *   *

As she worked on "The Dance of the Mother," going over and over the same slow motions, the stumbling, the reaching out, the empty-handedness, Leona began to feel that the gestures themselves were creating grief in her, a grief she had never known. Even when the rehearsal was over, she felt as if that new grief was still hanging on—in her, over her. She was out in the regular world, smiled, made small talk, laughed when she needed to laugh. But she was still caught in that whatever—it—was, that darkness. It made her feel a stranger to herself as well as to everybody else. It'll go away, it's probably what happens when you perform, she told herself.

One night, without warning, Aleida turned on her. "I've been working and working with you and nothing is happening," she yelled. "All you're doing is going through the motions. You're supposed to be showing us grief—remember? It's not a dance of the flowers."

"But I am feeling grief."

"It's not coming across as grief. And if it's not coming across as grief, you're not feeling it as grief. The whole thing is too loose, too soft, too mushy. It's without energy. It's got no life in it."

"But Ralph told me I was supposed to move as if I didn't quite realize what was happening to me, as if I was almost unable to move, as if my legs felt like lead, to be heavy—"

"He said to feel the weight of sorrow pulling you down. It's heavy. You've not. Incidentally," Aleida arched her long neck, "while we're on the subject of heaviness, there's something I've been wanting to say to you. Part

40

of the problem is the way you look. You've been putting on weight, just these past couple of weeks, and putting it on in the worst possible place, in your breasts and in your belly. But your legs are still so thin. It looks really weird. You're not pregnant, are you?"

"No, I'm not pregnant."

Still half in and half out of that darkness, Leona could make no sense of what was happening to her. She put her hands on her breasts. She looked down at her legs. Am I that fat and that weird looking? I can't have changed that much since rehearsals started. Could I have?

When she got home, later that night, everything in the house looked dirty, shabby, neglected. Suddenly she felt desperate. She went to the closet and got out the vacuum cleaner and began to clean the couch frantically.

Norman came out of the bedroom. "What are you doing, vacuuming at midnight?"

"I'm trying to get the cat hairs off," she said.

"Do it tomorrow," he said. "Come on, come to bed now."

"I—I—"

"What?" he said.

"Nothing." She wanted to tell him what had happened, but she couldn't say to him—to anyone—what Aleida had said. Those cruel words. If she repeated them, they would have even more power over her, they would become like glue, sticking to the grief, making a joke of all protection. I won't listen, she thought, but she could not not listen.

She went to bed and she and Norman had sex. She did not feel what she usually felt, that infinite capacity for absorption. There was that new grief between them, it absorbing, it like a yawning hole, empty of everything but the sensation of hurt. Almost at once her period began with a great gushing of blood. It's only that, she told herself, it's only my period that has made me feel this way, I should have known better.

* * *

In the morning when she came into the kitchen, she heard the children giggling. "Did you see the way she waddles?" Zack snickered.

"Why are you talking about me that way?" she yelled.

"We weren't talking about you, Mom," said Natalie.

"Yes you were. Do you think I'm too dumb to know?"

"We were talking about Felicity. Didn't you see how her stomach is hanging down? She's going to have kittens again."

They were talking about me, Leona knew.

12

The stage, brightly lit, was empty. At the back of the auditorium, waiting for the call for the dancers to rehearse, I sat, waiting.

All that had happened and not happened in the tryout for "The Dance of the Mother" was fading. It was a mem-

ory I could do without (particularly that bizarre movement that had come back again, on its own, unasked for).

No, I was not going to dwell on that. When you are
obligated to protect others, when that is your primary
obligation—when you have willingly chosen to protect
them—you are also obligated to protect yourself, not to
take any unnecessary risk. Uncertainty, dread, self-
revulsion—they are jeopardy for those who depend on
you, as well as nightmare for yourself.

But it was silly to think of this production as nightmare. I had been given a place in the chorus. So I didn't
get the solo part. I didn't want the solo part. Being in
the chorus was easy, it was without anxiety, it was without
risk. With the other women I danced the daily motions
of women of an earlier time working in a house. We
sewed, we washed, we cooked, we dusted, in large stylized
motions. Ralph's idea, Aleida said, is to show work as
pleasure. So keep it light and easy. When you're washing
and scrubbing, don't bear down, don't struggle.

The steps we were given to do were not subtle or sur-
prising. They were not—serious. But why did everything
have to be serious? They were, simply, pleasurable. There
is that in me, I decided, that I almost never pay attention
to, that is in favor of just plain pleasure.

I was pleased with the simple rhythmic steps, the light
skipping and sliding and small leaping. I was pleased
with the old-fashioned costume, a cotton dress with a
long full skirt. I was pleased with Raymond, my partner
in the waltz, a dance that Ralph had just recently inserted
in the production. Raymond was a thin, nervous man,
who waltzed well and always lifted me in the turn at
precisely the right moment. He and I never talked about
anything but the dance, about placement or timing. As
soon as the rehearsal was over, he always rushed off to
attend to other matters. Yet there was something pleasurable in this dancing with someone that you didn't

know, that you never even talked to. Here in this play without a plot—or without a plot that anyone, except maybe Ralph, could make out—I was finally beginning to let go.

13

Sounds of hammering came from offstage. Two stagehands appeared, carrying a long wooden box, which they set upright at the front center of the stage. Ralph entered from the wings. "You sure this is going to work?"

"No problem," one of them said. "She can get in and out of it easily."

"And it's not too heavy for the two men to carry?"

"It's a cinch," the other stagehand said. "They just have to remember to lift from the knees."

"You better be right," Ralph grumbled. "I don't want anyone getting any hernias."

"No one's going to get any hernias."

The stagehands went back into the wings but Ralph remained staring at the box, his body slumped into dejection or thought. A woman with long black hair, wearing a black costume appeared onstage.

"I'm not ready yet, Aleida," Ralph said with irritation.

He stood with his head bowed, slumped even further. "It's not right. It's not working."

"The box?"

"No, not the box. The scene. The whole thing is flat. It's got no life in it. It's heavy, it's—"

"But I thought you said—"

"I know what I said, you don't have to tell me." He banged his fist on the wooden box. "We're going to do it once more, and if it doesn't work any better, I'm going to take it out of the show."

"Take it out?" asked Aleida in panic. "Take out my solo? Five days before we open?"

"If necessary, I'll make changes up to the moment we open. We're going to get this thing right. Do you understand? Do you all understand?" he thundered at the actors who had assembled on the stage.

When he had finished speaking, there was silence. After a moment he asked mildly, "Any questions? No? No questions? Then we'll take it from the top." He jumped off the stage and walked back to a seat on the opposite side of the auditorium from where I was sitting.

*   *   *

The action on the stage began in darkness. A light came up on Aleida, turning in place, till she was going faster and faster, a whirling dervish in black on a small platform. Slowly the lights came up on the others. They were an audience, watching a performance that Aleida— or rather the dark woman—was giving. Suddenly two men jumped up from their seats. They began to utter cries and groans as they moved toward her. They grabbed her and dragged her off the platform, then lifted her into the open box at the rear of the stage. They shut the lower half-door of the box so only her upper body was visible. She could be seen beating upon the inner walls of the box with her hands. She tried to force her way out through the opening, but was thrust back by the two men. And all the time the audience—on the stage—sat in their seats, unmoving. What was supposed to be going on? It was clear that Aleida was supposed to be a hostage of some sort. But what was her relationship to those two men? And why did the rest of the audience go on regarding it as a performance? Was it a performance? There was something about Aleida in that box, battering to get out, that was malevolent, something animallike, no, less than animal, capable of deliberate cruelty, alive with rancor—yet personal somehow. It wasn't the way it had been with Ralph when he had done that movement of grief. With him it was as if a shell had dropped away and another being had emerged. As if it wasn't Ralph at all who was doing the moving. Later, when the movement was over, he went back to being the ordinary Ralph. But with Aleida it was different. It was as if she, Aleida, was doing the battering, as if she herself was growing larger to fill this woman, whose darkness was entirely at odds with what one would expect in this, in any play.

14

"Can I talk to you for a minute, someplace private?" It was Leona, leaning over in the dark, whispering, secretive.

I got up and followed her out of the auditorium, into the lobby, and down the narrow stairway. I noticed how awkwardly she moved as she descended. And she was chosen instead of me, the thought came to me, sharply, taking me by surprise with its bitterness.

Sinks on one side and stalls on the other, Leona faced me on the white hexagonally tiled floor of the rest room. She smiled faintly. She twisted her hands. She asked after the children, she asked after Gregg, she said we must all get together. She bit her lips then stood with her mouth agape.

"I," she burst out, "I—I thought I was showing grief. I thought I was feeling grief. But she says it's not grief." She began to cry. She kept trying to wipe the tears away with the back of her right hand. "I don't even know why I'm here—in this theater. I'm not a performer."

"Leona, none of us are really performers."

"But I—I'm— Every move I make she tells me is no good. She's always after me. She knew, they both knew what I was like. I'm not quick, I'm not skinny. They saw the way I moved before they chose me. So why did they choose me?" The tears ran down the side of her nose. "I can't do anything to please her."

Listening to Leona's words, I felt pleasure rise up in me. It was not a plain pleasure. It was like vengeance for a past hurt, but what was the hurt? It was gratification that the one who had been chosen was not pleasing, was not pleased.

But almost immediately this indecent pleasure—for it was indecent—gave way to sympathy, to the automatic impulse to put oneself in the place of the other, or at least to try to see with the other's eyes. I found myself urgently wanting to smooth things over, to defuse any argument or unpleasantness.

"She's probably on edge about the performance. Everybody's on edge. It doesn't really mean anything—"

"She says I'm not right for the part. Maybe I should just quit."

"If you talk to her—"

"I can't talk to her. I've tried—"

At that moment the door opened and Aleida came in. She was in her black costume but she had taken off her black wig. Her light brown hair was pinned up tightly in a bun. She raised her eyebrows, widened her eyes, and went into one of the stalls.

Leona turned to the mirror and looked at her swollen face. She turned on the cold water and put her hands, palms cupped, under the stream, then leaned over and bathed her face.

Through the opening below the metal door, I saw how Aleida's feet were set firmly on the floor. I heard the sound of flushing, the covering over of bodily sounds. (It is only Aleida, Aleida without a black wig, Aleida with her long torso and short muscular legs, shorter in proportion than they should be, like everyone else imperfect, like everyone else capable of shame, a woman who sits on a toilet and flushes first so the other sounds will not be heard.)

Aleida flushed the toilet again. She came out of the stall, she went to the sink and washed her hands. She shook the water off. She went over to the roller towel and pulled it down, once, then twice, and dried her hands. She came back to the sink and started unpinning her hair.

In the mirror I saw Aleida shaking out her hair.

"Either of you have a comb?" she asked.

"No," I said.

In the mirror I saw Leona looking at Aleida, I saw her open her mouth, but no words came out, I saw Leona turn to me—to my reflection in the mirror—as if she were saying, Help me, help me.

And I could not refuse.

"I think, Aleida, that you should know that Leona's upset."

"Upset? What do you mean upset?" Aleida was still looking at her image in the glass.

Yes, no, don't, maybe, I saw Leona shake her head in the mirror.

"She's talking about leaving the play."

"Leave? She must be kidding. Leave now, when I've spent all this time working with her on her part—when we're going to open in five days? What's the matter with her?"

"I told you, she's upset because—"

"Maybe she thought it was all going to be fun and games. Did you? Is that what you thought?" she turned furiously on Leona.

"I—I—I didn't think it would be like this. I thought it would be different. I didn't think you'd keep telling me that I'm stupid, that I can't move, that I'm fat."

Aleida turned back to the mirror, looked at me—at my

reflection—and shrugged. "I never said anything like that."

In the mirror I saw Leona, her head down, looking miserably at the tiled floor. I saw Aleida combing her hair with her fingers. I felt myself thicker at the waist, narrower at the shoulders.

"Why do you think I picked you for the part, Leona?" Aleida asked. There was a new note in her voice now, an edge of cajolery. "I picked you because Ralph—and I—thought you were right for it. The only thing is you're going to have to let go more into the character, into the feeling of the dance."

"I can't let go if you keep yelling at me, if every time I take a step, you tell me how terrible I look."

"I never said you looked terrible. I've just been pushing you for your own good. I want you to give the best performance you're capable of giving. What good would it do me or you if I pretended it was all right, when it wasn't right?"

"But you said I'm too fat."

"Oh, come on, Leona, we're all too fat. Me, you, even Anna. I could lose a few pounds in my hips, myself." She pounded her right hip with her hand and laughed.

"But what if I can't do it right?"

"You can do it. I know you can. I told you, all you have to do is let go. Listen, I don't have the time now to talk about it. I have to get back upstairs. They'll think I fell into a hole."

She opened the door. "Are you two coming? We're going to go through the first act again."

"I'll be up in a minute," I said.

As the two of them went out the door, I felt myself bodiless, without substance or weight, as if I existed only for others' purposes, as if I were nothing but a catalyst, an intermediary, an audience for others' lives.

15

After Rebecca and Amy were asleep, I went into the bedroom and stood in front of the full-length mirror. Were those new lines about my eyes? I saw the dark hair, the skin sallow in the overhead light, the body not quite thin enough. I stared at the figure. It stared back, the confirmation of how one could dissipate oneself before others, how one could lose oneself in the sight of others, dissolve in and into their sight—as if eyes were holes for swallowing, as if eyes were active agents of motion, reaching out, capable of consuming.

In a sweat I opened the closet and pulled out a new black dress with triangular cutouts around the neck. I tried it on, I took it off. From the closet I pulled a beige dress with a cowl neckline. I tried it on, I took it off. I kept on pulling out, trying on, taking off—first this, then that—a purple tweed skirt flecked with black, a purple silk shirt, a sundress with blue and green vertical stripes, one garment after the other, till I had emptied almost the entire closet. The clothes lay about me in heaps, the aftermath of a frenzy of clothing an image which nothing seemed to fit. Everything I owned seemed old, worn, graceless, askew, inappropriate—not right. My eyes looked back at me mournfully. But I wasn't mournful, I had no justification for mourning. If Gregg were here, this wouldn't have happened. Alone—with the children—alone, I exaggerated everything. Things took a crazy course. Revulsion had no boundaries. For I felt revulsion now, at myself, at how I looked—

I hung the clothes in the closet, I took a hot shower, I went to bed.

*　*　*

I dreamed I saw a child climbing on a massive black rock at the edge of the sea. From the shore I waved to him in greeting. The child did not wave back, he was engrossed in the climbing. The tide was rising, but he was not aware of it. I called out to him in warning, but he did not respond, he kept on climbing. I called out his name, shouting it again and again. But even as I called to him, it seemed strange to me that I should call this boy, whose safety I was somehow responsible for, by his last name. The water rose higher and I awoke to my own moaning.

I strained to listen in the silence. There was a creaking of wood, a snap somewhere, but no sound from the children's room. I was possessed by a great fear for them. We were all in jeopardy. In a moment the whole world could shatter, could fall into no time, all time, into no place, all place.

In the gray light I struggled to reach the surface of the familiar: the steady birch dresser (with a mar upon it, where I had spilled the perfume that was a present from Gregg on our last anniversary), the white drapes that covered the wall of windows, the photos on the opposite wall, the straight black chair in the corner. And there in the corner, a small huddled animal. No—it was only my black sweater, one of the things I had tried on last night, somehow overlooked when I was putting things away.

I thought of last night's frenzy with a small shame, a bit of contempt. There are certain memories—of images or actions, distant or near—that can and should be erased. (No, I no longer feel that way. Yes, I was a fool to feel—to see—that way.) So I felt when I looked at the thing on the floor.

I knew in the morning light what mattered. The real life, the important life was this daily one with the children and Gregg, the one that marked my clear responsibility, where sight was never a matter of choice, but memory was.

Memory, after all, was an indulgence based upon too simple suppositions about cause and effect, when what mattered, what really mattered here in this room was Amy who had just come in trailing her blanket, getting into bed wordlessly, cuddling up against me.

"What do you want for breakfast this morning?"

And then Amy's usual answer. "I don't want breakfast."

And then the play of horror: "No breakfast?"

And then the shaking of the head. No. No.

And then, threateningly, the voice of the ogre: "You've got to have breakfast."

And then Amy, shaking her head, "I'm too young for breakfast," laughing, loving repetition.

16

Yes, I said to myself, I will remember what matters when I am at the Community Theater. I will take that production, that play, for what it really is: a small thing, an interlude, of no profound importance. For pleasure, only for pleasure.

So I thought, so I warned myself as I went those last few evenings to the final rehearsals, while Gregg stayed at home with the children.

There was an excitement among us—dancers, singers, and actors. There was a sense of camaraderie, of instant and intimate community. We were all working together, helping each other, the dissensions, whatever they were, covered over, all in the service of a good performance, to please the audience that was to come.

Even Ralph seemed calmer, no longer demanding that this be changed, that that be changed. But, as it turned out, it was only the calm before the final storm.

*   *   *

"No, no, no," Ralph began to yell. We were in the final dress rehearsal, in the next to the last scene.

"What's happened to you all? Where's the liveliness? Where's the freshness? Where's the vitality? You look like a bunch of old women, dragging yourself here, dragging yourself there. Let's have a little pep. Let's give it a little oomph. You," he pointed to me, "I want you to be a little kid in this scene, over here on the side, near this tree."

"Like this?" I said, "Wearing this? How can I be a little kid in this long cotton dress?"

"You can go downstairs and get a little girl's costume and a blond wig—with curls. That's no problem. No, not now. Later," he yelled as I started to leave. "I want you here right now, right here, right next to this tree."

I went over to the spot he'd pointed to. He came up to me. I felt a small revulsion at the sly sloppiness of his face so close to mine. I could see the sweat above his upper lip. I could see the broken veins in his skin. He took me by the shoulders and moved me nearer to the tree. It was made of heavy cardboard, set on a small round base. The tree was painted a tree only on the side facing the audience.

"Now, let's go through it again," he called out, "from the top."

"What am I supposed to do?" I said. I could hear the tightness in my throat. "Just stand here?"

"Jump around a little, hop a little, skip a little," he said blandly. "Make a couple of turns. Do whatever you want to do, just as long as you look like a little kid having a great time. You know, 'Happy Days of Childhood,' that sort of thing. Okay," he turned to the rest of the cast, "this applies to all of you. Lightness, not heaviness. Take the lead out of your pants."

*   *   *

For the first three performances I did what Ralph asked of me. I jumped, I skipped, I was like a little kid having a good time in my kid's costume. The curls on my blond wig bounced, I bounced, I was carefree, it was all very pleasurable. But then the night of the fourth and final performance, when I took my place beside the tree and began to hop and to skip, I felt suddenly a resentment so fierce that I could hardly make myself move. I felt the pressure, the weight of that resentment like a burden upon my back. I felt I was being held down. I felt that the pleasure of this child I was supposed to be had never been my pleasure. I felt heaviness and a small dread. I tried to smile as I had smiled in the earlier performances. I tried to make myself look happy, even joyous, but the muscles on my face had stiffened, just as I had stiffened. I wrenched myself into moving, even though moving was like pushing my way through thickness, through murkiness. I had to move, I was expected to move. Out there were others watching me, waiting. I had no choice but to move. I began to turn in a circle (that thing was still on my back weighing me down). I turned faster, then faster, trying to throw it off. I was like a whirling dervish in my turning, but still it held on. My turn became a kicking turn, flailing, lashing out. Each time I spun around my foot came out harder, sharper. I felt myself moving, I felt myself being moved. I had almost recaptured pleasure.

Then my foot, lashing out, hit the painted tree. I was aware, even as I kept on turning, that the tree was spinning, that now it was wobbling, that now it had ended up with its unpainted side to the audience.

With the others I ran into the wings. I saw Ralph. He was bearing down on me. "Go out there and turn that tree around!" he said quietly, though I could see how the veins around his nose, on his cheeks, were standing out, larger, redder.

56

I stood there unmoving. "The audience has already seen the unpainted side. It would make it worse to turn it around again," I said.

"I said get out there and turn it around," he repeated. His lips were like two thin lines.

"It will just remind them that it's all an illusion," I said, stubbornly.

"Don't be smart ass with me," Ralph hissed so loud, he must have been heard by the audience.

"I'll do it," Leona said, and she slipped out on stage and quietly, slowly, turned the tree around.

17

Under a sun, brilliant but not hot, the edges of the buildings in town, ocher and sand-colored, vibrated against the blue of the sky. The colors of the yard trees thrust themselves forward—the red in the toyon, the green in the pine, the blue-gray of the eucalyptus. Looking up from the valley, one saw the dark jagged line of trees outlining the ridge.

The cold—cold, that is, for Peralta—brought with it the reminder that the world was clearly demarcated between inside and outside. Doors and windows were shut. Outside, sounds seemed harder, sharper, more metallic, as if transmitted through a medium thinner than air. Inside, sounds seemed softer, sheltering.

* * *

With the radiant heat in the floor turned way up, Leona padded around the house barefoot. She made herself coffee, she looked at the morning paper, at the headlines, at the funnies, at the ads. She thought about getting dressed.

Now that the performance was over and evenings were her own, she felt she could once again do everything slowly, at her pace. With Norman at work and the children at school, she could, if she felt like it, flop for a moment on the white couch. Nobody was here to direct her as to when she should do this and when she should do that. Through the floor-to-ceiling windows she looked out on the garden. A newly planted bed of geraniums stood blackened and shriveled from the frost. But inside, inside her house, she was like a hothouse plant, nurtured, protected.

She stretched and shifted on the couch. She felt the giving softness beneath her, molding to her shape. It pleased her to think that when she got up, there would be an indentation of herself still lying there. I should get up, she thought. Ninta's class was that afternoon. But no, she did not want to go to Ninta's class. She didn't know when she would go back, if ever. Now all she wanted to do was to bask in her sense of the wave after wave of applause enveloping her as she took the final curtain call.

Earlier there had been all that doubt and grief—that false grief. She had wept in front of Anna and Aleida. But then it had all changed. Aleida, who had seemed so mean before, had turned out to be an angel. Not once during the rest of the rehearsals did she say anything harsh. In fact she was always encouraging, praising her before the others. And finally, with Aleida's help, she had been able to do "The Dance of the Mother" as it should have been done. Everybody did so well, it was a great success. Only Anna, steady, reliable Anna, had done that crazy thing.

That last night—Leona was standing in the wings so she'd seen it all—as Anna was turning next to the tree, suddenly she speeded up and her movements started getting larger and sharper. Why is she doing that? Leona had wondered. It didn't look like "Happy Days of Childhood" any more. It looked more like a whirling maniac. She tried to signal Anna to go slower, but Anna kept on going faster and faster, kicking, until finally she'd hit that tree and it wobbled, ending wrong side front. She should have fixed it when Ralph told her to fix it. Why didn't she do that? It was no big deal.

Leona stretched and patted Felicity, who was lying beside her, leaving more black cat hairs on the white couch. Running her hand over the black fur, Leona saw how gray it was becoming near the skin. But Felicity wasn't that old. She was only—what?—six?—eight?

I should get up, Leona said to herself. But the thought of the cold outside and the warm inside made her feel so sultry, so relaxed. She smiled, remembering when she was a child, how she would lie on the old green couch in the living room and her mother would say, Why don't you go out and play? But Leona knew her mother really wasn't angry with her, really didn't mind her hanging about, even as she herself flew about in a frenzy of cleaning. It was as if she, Leona, was the still warm center around which everything revolved.

18

The wind sought out the cracks in the old cottage. It blew out the paper shades, so they billowed like sails. No matter how many clothes Aleida put on, she was always cold. Not even her rage could keep her warm.

For she was full of rage now. A rage at Ralph, a rage at all that let Leona triumph, a triumph that she had helped Leona to achieve while she herself lost. Yes, she had helped Leona and been nice to her, but she'd had to grit her teeth while she was doing it. She had never wanted Leona for the part in the first place but Ralph had insisted, saying, I know she's the right one. Aleida knew Ralph would have held her responsible if Leona left, and then he would have taken away her own solo.

But as it was—she could still hardly believe it—at the very last minute he had done just that. Or he might just as well have, the way he changed it so that it was nothing but a ridiculous interlude. He took out the box, he took out the audience watching her on stage. He told her to jump from spot to spot as if she were being pursued over some ice floes. What had he had in mind? He never made it clear. She herself had only gone through the motions with a kind of disgust. But meantime, she had helped Leona . . .

She got some masking tape out, and taped the shades to the wooden frames around the windows, so they wouldn't flap. Then she got out some old blankets and she put them over the windows, securing them with thumbtacks and nails. It seemed to help with the cold, though now the rooms were dark even in the daytime, and of course she couldn't see out. She didn't care, the world could all go to hell as far as she was concerned.

I should never have gone back when my mother told me to go back, she told herself as she lay on the couch, feeling the blanket wrinkle beneath her. But what choice did I have? She would have made me go back anyway. What I should have done—only I didn't think of it then— once I was in the line, I should have done everything wrong, everything out of step or backwards. So, if we were supposed to go right, I should have gone left. Then he would have yelled at me, Wrong way, what's the matter with you? And I would have acted innocent and surprised. Or if we were supposed to do something in double time, I should have gotten the tempo all wrong, done it in half-time or even slower. And he would have yelled, Wrong time. And I would have looked confused and done the same thing again. And he would finally have said, I can't keep you in the show, you're making too many mistakes.

That, at least, would have been the beginning of getting away.

19

Each time I came into the living room I smelled a strange smell. It was one of those smells that came and went. The moment you tried to pinpoint it, it was gone. But one morning, as I was vacuuming, I noticed that the corner of one of the cork tiles of the living room floor was lifting up. I bent down and lifted it further and saw that just beneath the cork tile the concrete was moist. It smelled of mold.

The plumber came, he looked, he felt the dampness, he shook his head. You've got a leak all right. It's probably in the radiant heat system. That's big trouble. The pipes are in the cement slab and getting to them is going to be a real pain in the neck. I've seen it once before, in one other house in the tract. The problem is the builder used iron pipe with a plastic coating instead of copper pipe because copper was expensive and hard to get. When they laid the pipe, in some places the coating got scraped away. The pipe corroded and there's your leak.

Can it be fixed? Better have your husband call me. It'll be expensive. I'll have to tear up the floor and drill into the slab and replace the corroded pipe. The only problem is, it's hard to find out just where the leak is. It could be under that tile but then again it could be anywhere in the system, anywhere in the slab, and just surfacing there.

Bad luck, he added, as he left. Maybe you should sue the builder. Only thing, you probably won't win. And even if you win, by the time you get it settled, the house won't be standing. These houses aren't built the way they used to be in the old days.

When Gregg got home, I told him what had happened and he called the plumber. I think we should just wait and see what happens, he said when he hung up. The leak either will or won't get worse. If it doesn't get worse, we'll ignore it. And if it does get worse, it will probably be easier to locate it.

Ignore it? I didn't know how to ignore it.

Every time I came into the living room I was sure I smelled the smell more. I felt that there was something profoundly wrong. I had the feeling that the very foundation of the house was giving way. I knew it was only a matter of leaking pipes, of a wet concrete slab, but it felt to me as if I were standing in water which was rising and rising—no matter how slowly—till one day it—the house—myself—and everything in it would be engulfed.

20

Suddenly, perhaps it was because of the unusual cold, Norman expressed the desire to go ice dancing. He, who had never cared about anything but his job, now wanted to go three times a week, leaving work an hour early to drive the thirty miles to the ice rink.

Where he got the idea about ice dancing Leona didn't know, but not only did he want it for himself, he insisted that she go with him and the kids too. She went, the kids went, they all rented skates. She got out on the ice, she fell and fell again. Her ankles kept turning in toward each other as if they longed for some support stronger than air. Norman, zooming by, stopped and picked her up, said, Don't stop, you'll get the hang of it, keep practicing. Then he skated off and left her, wobbling.

But the rink was too cold, the sounds of metal and music were too harsh. How glad she was when it was time to leave. As they all piled into the car, Norman said, Wasn't that great? We're really getting out of the old routine. The thought came to Leona that this was only a new routine but she held back, she did not say it to him.

As soon as they got home, she said she was too tired to make dinner, they should all fend for themselves. Exhausted and chilled, she went to bed right away. She dreamed that she was in a house that was strange to her, yet she knew it was her house. A big party was going on. She was so tired she went into the bedroom and lay on the bed. But it was so noisy, she could get no rest. Aleida entered, with five or six followers. They all went to the corner, then each one in turn took a running jump and flew up from the floor and around the room. In the dream Leona thought, Isn't this strange? But no, it's not strange, she corrected herself, it's plain to see that they are being carried by the air. Looking up, she felt a piercing envy at their lightness.

She woke to the sounds of laughter, the kids laughing and Norman laughing too. She could hear the exuberance in his laugh, as if he had just solved some critical problem, as if he were wandering again in his "fields." He loves the ice dancing, the kids love it, but I hate it. So why am I going? Because I'm a puppet, the thought came to her. I am—have been—a puppet. I only move when others have forced me to move. I have not—ever— really moved myself.

21

Once again things were as they had been in Peralta. The cold wave—such as it was—passed. Doors and windows were once again open to the soft, benign air; children ran freely in and out.

Now, suddenly, Leona began to worry about money. All she kept thinking was, What will the company think, What will his boss say? For Norman was now going ice dancing five days a week, leaving work each day at three.

"Aren't they going to get mad at you for leaving so early?"

"So let them fire me."

"But what will we live on?" she said in a panic. It was the thought of money moving within her, moving now with urgency. (How swiftly thoughts of money move within the slow moving.)

"I'll get another job."

"Is it that easy to get one, just like that?"

"If not here, I can get one back East."

"And give up the house?"

"How come you're so attached to the house all of a sudden?"

"I was always attached to the house."

"You couldn't tell from the way you take care of it."
She was about to say she took care of it in her own way,
when suddenly he burst out, "If you were only capable
of a little self-discipline—"

She tried to remain quiet, not to provoke him, but in
fact it was her quiet that provoked him.

"All I'm asking for is a certain amount of consideration," he yelled, "from you and the kids. Is that so much
to ask—that you all—for a change—do things the way I
want them done—for a change."

"What is the matter with you? You're dissatisfied with
everything. Me. The kids. The house. Everything but ice
dancing. Why are you blaming us? Is there something
wrong at work?"

"Something wrong at work? How could anything be
wrong at work," he said mockingly. Then bitterly he cried
out, "I'll tell you what's wrong at work. They're going
into production on the new machine, *my* new machine,
that's what's happening. They've used my ideas but I'm
not getting a thing out of it."

"You told me yourself that your name was on the patent."

"Everybody else's name is on it too. It doesn't mean a
thing. The real question is who's getting the money? The
company is getting the money. And people like Gregg
are getting the power. And what do I get? Nothing." He
sat on the couch and put his head in his hands.

It frightened her to see him look so lost. "Can't I do
anything to help you?"

"What can you do, Leona? You can hardly do what
you have to do here. Everything is too much for you."

"It's not. I could go to work. I've been thinking of going to work. The kids are older, I have spare time."

"Spare time," he said. "You have spare time all right,
to be in a performance, to go to your dance classes—"

"I thought you wanted me to do that," she wailed. "I

would never have done it otherwise. You said I should be getting out more, moving more—"

Still he sat with his head in his hands. She took a deep breath. "So I won't go to the dance classes any more, if it makes you feel better."

"I don't care. Go if you like. What difference does it make?"

Yet even though they argued, that night, like every other night, they made love. What happened to the argument in sex, she didn't exactly know. It was blotted out in the motion of his needing, of his wanting, of his being drawn inside her.

22

Leona went out to look for a job. (What it is to make yourself move, when you only want to stay in place.) It was hard enough to make a telephone call to ask about an opening, let alone get dressed and go out to the interview to be rebuffed and rebuffed again. But finally she did find something, a job as an assistant to the technicians in the medical laboratory in town.

The first day, Bob, the senior technician, instructed her in her duties. She was so fearful that she would not get everything right, she wrote what he said on a pad of paper and kept checking that she had not forgotten any-thing. The next morning she arrived earlier than she was supposed to, to be sure to get things ready. Several times she made a mistake but Bob was not impatient. You'll get it, it takes time, he said. It was so hard, there were so many things to remember to do in an exact sequence. She wondered if she would ever get it right.

Nevertheless, it was as Bob had said. It only took time. Going over and over the same things day after day did make a difference. Soon she felt confident, soon she was even taking comfort in the routine, in the exactness of repetition. Now and then, when she was home in the evening and Norman was out ice dancing, she would think about the oddness of the blood in the vials. How hard it was to imagine that this was what ran through veins and arteries, this was what hearts pumped, this red, this liquid. (Did Bob say it was blue inside?) When it was inside you, you couldn't feel the blood moving. And once it was outside, it was hard to believe it had ever been inside. Though of course it had been. You could see it, coming out of the arms of the patients as they sat with the tight bands about their upper arms, some looking at the blood flowing out into the vials and some looking away. And she thought of herself and her own inner blood that spilled out of her monthly, sometimes in too great a rush so that she had to wear two pads at a time.

23

"In this improvisation," said Ninta, "we will depart from what we've done before. I've often spoken to you about internal monitoring. This will be an exploration of external monitoring. Each of you will work with a partner."

She paired us off. "Start out by facing each other. One will begin to move, then the other will try to match that motion exactly—in time and in space. It's tricky, you'll see, so work slowly. I suggest that the one moving start with a simple gesture. After you become more accustomed to this process of reflecting and being reflected, you can go on to a movement phrase, or possibly even a sequence of several phrases."

I turned to my partner, Aleida.

"I'll start," Aleida said.

Even before she began to move, I anticipated in my own body what she would do. I recalled the way Aleida had moved before. The sensual line, the suggestion of travesty, that darkness on stage, the pounding of her hip, her feet planted on the floor of the stall as she had flushed (No, that wasn't motion)—But here, now, in this improvisation, Aleida was careful, controlled, limiting herself to simple basic gestures—a lean to the side, a lift on half-toe.

Warily I followed her, one phrase at a time, following her every motion with my eyes, at the same time sensing, surmising, even knowing ahead of time, how the movement would develop and come to completion.

"Now," said Ninta, "change off. The one leading becomes the one following."

I began with a simple motion, a twist in the upper body to the left, a return to the center, a twist in the upper body to the right, a return to the center. Be careful, I said to myself, seeing how Aleida was watching me so closely, remembering how Aleida had laughed at me, at that motion in class before—wasn't it Aleida?— remembering how Aleida had looked in the mirror in the bathroom at the Community Theater, how she was the kind who could pretend niceness if it was necessary, all the time for her own purposes, taking over. That was what she was, one of those who took over.

Carefully, warily, I did a series of phrases, restrained, cautious, which Aleida followed tenaciously, never missing a beat or a step.

But what could be taken here? It was only a movement, a gesture in a dance class.

"Change again," said Ninta.

24

The annual Peralta picnic was held on a ranch off a narrow winding road high in the hills above town. The road from the ranch gate followed a steep slope down to a wide grassy meadow. From there hill upon lower hill sloped down to the valley.

An old Peralta family had deeded the property to the city, to be kept in its native state. Only for the community picnic were any structures allowed on the land and these were temporary. At one end of the meadow, next to a pony ring, a tent had been set up for a puppet show for the children. At the other end were wooden booths with food and things to be sold to promote community causes.

Walking out of the shade of the trees into the sunlit meadow, I came to the White Elephant booth. I thought I saw something blue glint in the sun. Half-hidden, under a pile of books and two porcelain shepherdesses with broken crooks, I found a blue shawl. The way the metallic spangles glittered reminded me of a costume I had wanted to wear but had not worn when I was a child.

I pulled the shawl out, held it up, and examined it for flaws, then wrapped it around my shoulders. I looked up and saw two girls behind the wooden counter, absorbed in conversation. A man was leaning casually against the endpost of the booth, his blond hair luminescent in the sunlight.

"Looks good," he said.

"How much is it?" I asked one of the girls.

"Fifty cents. Everything's fifty cents."

I took the coins out of my purse, hesitated, then folded the shawl and put it back beneath the shepherdesses. The man was still watching me, his eyes an intense blue beneath the shock of bright hair. His nose was flattened at the bridge, giving his even-featured face a hint of regret or vexation.

"You should get it. It suits you."

"No, I don't think it's for me." I turned and walked away.

"Wait a minute," he said. I kept on walking.

"Why do you look so angry?" he said, as he caught up with me.

"I'm not angry."

"What's your hurry?"

"I'm going to pick up my children. They're watching the puppet show."

"Mind if I walk with you?"

I shrugged. I kept walking; he was still following me. I felt I couldn't shake him off without making a scene. I didn't want to make a scene. I didn't want to be looked at by a crowd of strangers.

He didn't say anything, he just walked beside me. It made me nervous. But I wasn't going to make conversation for conversation's sake.

We came to the puppet theater, a tent with the words "Punch and Judy" on a hand-painted sign tacked to the canvas. Through the tent opening came the sound of children's laughter.

"Once I saw a Punch and Judy show," he said. I thought

he was going to say something funny but his voice was tense, clogged, almost as if he didn't expect me to listen. "I was a little kid. Punch hit Judy and then Judy hit Punch. Then he hit her again and she hit him again. I didn't think it was funny. But everybody else was laughing so I made myself laugh. Everytime they laughed, I laughed. Then I found I was laughing even when they weren't laughing. I couldn't stop laughing. They all turned and looked at me. I thought it was crazy myself but I still couldn't stop laughing."

"I'm not sure I understand why you're telling me this."

"Why not?"

"I don't know. It just seems—"

"Does it offend you?"

"No, it doesn't offend me. Only—"

"Only what? It's not the sort of thing people say to each other at a community picnic?"

"It's not that but you hardly know me so why—"

"But I do know you," he said and grinned. "I've heard all about you." He grinned again. "From my wife." He gestured to where Aleida was standing with a group of others, her hands on her hips.

Seeing the long neck, seeing the sloping shoulders, seeing the toss of the head, I thought, Yes, Aleida, of course, Aleida.

I felt the muscles of my face trying to hold to rigidity, but giving way. I turned away from him so that he might not see the feelings following one upon the other, that I was surprised that this was Aleida's husband, that I wasn't surprised, why should I care, that I didn't care, that his very presence was irritating me, that I was pleased by his persistence, that, yes, I was sure, he was playing upon me in some way.

I smelled the smoke of the meat being barbecued across the meadow. I felt hunger and a small nausea.

74

The children began to stream out of the tent, some laughing, some talking, some silent.

"It was fun," said Rebecca, running over to me.

"I didn't like it," said Amy. "It was scary."

I picked Amy up and felt her head nestle against my shoulder. I turned my chin so it rested on her head. "Are you tired? Do you want to go home?" I asked her in a low voice.

"I want to go on the pony ride again," insisted Rebecca.

"I'm tired," said Amy. "I want to go home."

"Let Rebecca have one more ride and then we'll go."

"I want to go on the pony ride too," Amy said.

I put her down and she ran after Rebecca.

"I'll be in touch," he said, touching me on the shoulder where Amy had lain her head.

25

I had said yes. I did not know why I said yes.

It could not have been simply his charm, his charming seductiveness, that had persuaded me to come here with him.

Yet there I was, with him, about to enter Cabin Number Five of "The Belle View Motor Court." (Eight shabby cabins grouped around an even shabbier trailer with a vacancy sign propped in its window.)

Perhaps it had been when he had said, What would be the harm? that I had simply thought, What would be the harm?

No, I did not want harm. But no harm would come from this one time—to anyone. This had nothing to do with love. It had to do with tightening at the neck and not being able to let go. It had to do with wanting to leap out of the present, out of the confinement of space, out of the place I was in, to where motion of another sort would take me over.

From the adjacent highway I heard the sound of traffic, a constant hum and then a changing sound superimposed upon the steady one, higher then lower as the cars passed in speeding gusts.

The door was stuck and he had to fiddle with the key in the lock. I waited, shivering in the cool air. He shoved the door open and turned on the overhead light. Covering the bed, which was deeply sunken in the middle, was a pale yellow chenille spread. Through the open bathroom door I could see the edge of the peeling brown linoleum. There was a smell of mold in the room. I heard a truck go by, then another. I saw the flimsy straight chair, the unpainted wooden night table, the flaking green paint on the dresser, the worn and dirty gray rug.

I saw him turning to me in the too bright, too dim glare of the overhead bulb. (And I thought of that dance with a partner on the stage of the Community Theater, the dance with the man who was supposed to be my lover, a man I never knew at all, hardly even talked to, yet we had danced a dance of love together.)

I shivered again. "Are you cold?" he asked.

"No," I said. It was so ugly in the room, I did not think it would be so ugly.

"Not exactly what you'd call luxurious, is it?"

"No, it's not."

"But it is out of the way. You said you wanted it to be out of the way."

"Yes, it is out of the way."

"Do you want to leave? Do you want to go somewhere else?"

"No. No."

"Well then, as long as we're here," he said and laughed. He put his hand out to me. He took my hand. I looked into his face. A stranger.

*   *   *

Afterwards, he turned and lay with his arms outstretched. He was almost asleep. I had taken an action, perhaps I had always wanted to take this action, this motion that had propelled me and was still propelling me. My other life, the life I lived everyday—No, I would not think of it—of course, it was still going on, would still go on. But this was a parallel, an alternate life I'd leaped into. I'd fallen into another existence, and could, if I wanted to, turn and see myself as I always was, in place.

I put my hand up to touch his arm. I felt a rough place running from his elbow to his shoulder. He stirred and said, "An old scar."

"How—"

"It's nothing, it's not worth talking about."

I didn't press him. I liked the fact that he was someone detached from me, from my everyday life, someone with a secret history. I felt that I too was becoming someone with a secret history.

He put his arm under me and I moved to be closer to him. He winced. "Those earrings are sharp," he said. I took them off and laid them on the scratched night table. I moved close to him again.

I noticed that his eyes were on the ceiling and that he was holding his other hand up, making a curious motion, touching his thumb to one finger and then the next. He saw that I was looking at him and laughed charmingly, sheepishly. "I was counting the cracks in the ceiling."

"Why?"

"It's just a habit. Like some people have to put their pants on a certain way, first the right leg, then the left. You must have your habits."

"Yes, I guess."

"Tell me some of your habits," he said, turning over and leaning on his elbow, looking at me.

"Well, I—I—" I paused. "I hate habits," I said, lightly.

"You hate habits? How can you hate habits? Everybody's got habits. You couldn't live without habits."

I shrugged. "Did you ever try it?"

"But it's not possible."

"No, I guess it's not possible." I saw that he was looking at the ceiling again. "Once—" I said.

I began to tell him a story of my childhood, of when my family was living in a dark railroad flat and my father used to bring home pearl buttons from the factory where he worked. We—my mother and father and I—would sit around the dining room table, pushing long thin wires through the shanks of the buttons to test them. If the shanks had no holes, they had to be discarded or perhaps set aside for reboring. We were paid forty-three cents a box for doing this, and one box was twenty or forty gross. One box alone took several hours. I complained to my father that it was slave labor, but he shrugged and said, what did I know about slavery, at least it would bring in a little extra money for food and rent.

One night the ceiling above the table where we were working suddenly collapsed. Large and small pieces of plaster fell upon the table. White flakes, white powder, were now mixed in among all the white buttons, sorted and unsorted.

My father went downstairs to tell the super. The super came back upstairs with him. The super was a redheaded man with an Irish brogue. He looked up at the ceiling with the wooden slats showing bare, and then he looked down at the table with the buttons among the pieces of plaster.

And what are all those little buttons? Those are buttons, aren't they? he asked in his strong brogue.

Yes, they're buttons, my father said. It's just a game we play with buttons.

I felt a terrible shame, not only because of the lie, but perhaps just as much because the lie wasn't believed. Even then, by the way the superintendent grinned, I knew that he knew it was a lie.

Why am I telling him this? I wondered. For pity? No, I am not interested in being pitied. That was not what I wanted. I only wanted to say what had once been.

Now it was his turn to tell. "My father had a job in the paper mill in town. He'd been in the same job for years. Then one day they let him go, just like that. He was so angry he never worked again. My mother worked, all of us kids worked, but he refused, he just sat there in his chair, his large black chair in the living room, and he never moved out of it—until the day he died."

He turned and began to caress me, more urgently, I noticed, than before. The effect of stories? Of stories exchanged?

"Just a minute, wait a minute," I said and slipped out of his embrace, got up and took the tube of vaginal jelly from my purse and started toward the bathroom.

"You don't need to do that," he said.

"Why not?"

"I'm sterile."

I hesitated a moment. "How can you be sure?"

"I know. I've had a vasectomy."

I put the vaginal jelly back in my purse.

"Aleida wanted it and I figured why not."

A moment before I had had the sense that I was about to find out something crucial about him, as if he were about to open up his skin to me and say, Look what's underneath. But now he had put it back in place, he was saying, Don't look. Why should I look, I didn't want to look. A sense of loss, of regret, of pathos had crept into his voice, a tone that made me say to myself, Beware, he is playing on you, trying to make Aleida out to be the culprit and himself the victim.

Yet when he began to play upon my body, I could no longer distinguish victim, persecutor, the acted upon, the actor, nor did I care.

* * *

He sat up against the scuffed wall, the pillow behind him, and smoked a cigarette. Lying beside him in that ugly, seedy room, I found myself saying, "I feel so lucky."

"Lucky?" He smiled indulgently. "That's nice."

The word had come of itself but perhaps it was not the right word. "I don't mean lucky, exactly."

"What then, exactly?"

"Impersonal, maybe."

"Impersonal?"

"Yes, impersonal." I was intent on saying it exactly. "As if I were outside myself in some way, as if I weren't trapped by old feelings or false feelings . . ."

I saw that he looked bewildered but I thought, No, I won't stop, this is what I want, this is part of it, that I can go on and not worry about what he will say, this is part of that being impersonal, that I can start along a path and keep going, go further and further and not be impeded by old things, as if even talk had new forms, forms it was capable of but that had never been used.

I felt a rushing, a tingling, I felt transparent and expanded at the same time. Even this room, this ugly, seedy room, and the things in it, could take on another aspect, needn't be judged by ordinary vision, as if it could be looked at in another way, be seen through detached eyes ...

"Impersonal. It doesn't sound very complimentary," he said lightly.

"I'm just trying to be honest."

"Of course it's important to be honest."

"Yes."

He leaned over me and put out his cigarette in the black cracked ashtray. He pulled the sheets up over his chest. He leaned back against the pillow. "Have you told Gregg about us?"

I had not wanted to think about—had not been thinking about Gregg. "He's away. No, of course not. I wouldn't tell him."

"You don't want that kind of honesty?"

"No."

"Why not?"

Once again he was pushing me, just as he had pushed me when we first met and I had been so irritated with him. How had I forgotten that irritation? Now, looking at him, as he took out another cigarette, I thought, No, he is not charming, not charming at all.

Leaning against that scuffed wall, he too seemed scuffed, as if there were something sly and sneaky and cunning about him. He was counting the cracks in the ceiling again with his hands, his pudgy hands, saying, "I don't see any reason why people shouldn't tell each other. Not because of honesty but because of pleasure."

"Pleasure?"

"Yes, pleasure. I'm sure Aleida'd be pleased to know.

In fact, it was Aleida who pointed you out to me at the picnic, who pointed out how attractive you are."

In my body I felt that what was wet was growing dry, what was thick and smooth was growing thin and rough. Yet he, just at this moment, wanted to start again, began to caress me again.

I pushed him away. "What's the matter now?"

"I'm past pleasure," I said.

He laughed. "That's a funny thing to say, I mean funny peculiar, not funny ha-ha. Past pleasure," he repeated and he laughed again, a mocking laugh, a forced laugh, an imitation of a laugh.

I got out of bed and began to dress—steadily, surely.

"Don't go." It sounded like pleading. (Too late for pleading.) He reached out and took my hand.

"I have to go, it's getting late."

He dropped my hand. He jumped up and went past me into the bathroom. I heard the shower go on and with the sound began another louder one, a terrible knocking in the pipes. Knock, knock, knock, it shook the whole room. I should leave now, I should call a cab, I told myself. But there was no phone in the room and I certainly wasn't going to go into that grimy trailer and face who knew what grimy man or woman, snickering.

I began to shiver at the thought of what I had actually been risking—

The knocking in the pipes ended. He came out of the bathroom, his hair wet, his body still wet. I looked at him but I felt immune to him, as if he were an aberration, or a character in a story that had been told a long time ago, who was already hazy, half-forgotten.

I watched him, objectively, impersonally, as he dressed. He put the right pant leg on first and then the left. I turned away from him.

Yes, I had habits. I had a habit of throwing myself into darkness, I had a habit of making others larger to be the proof of my own smallness. Yes, I had a habit of thinking I was thinking, when it wasn't thought at all that I was caught up in but some feverish cycling of my nerves. I had a habit of being a fool. I had a habit of wasting my daring on the impossible.

In the silence I heard a truck pass and then another on the highway and I thought of those going by, bypassing the "Belle View Motor Court."

"You forgot your earrings," he said. I turned and watched him as he picked them up from the scarred table. I put out my hand.

He put the earrings in my palm.

"Be careful," he said. "You can draw blood with these."

26

Soon Leona was given the task of collecting the leftover blood from the technologists and disposing of it. Every day, so much blood—to pour out.

"It's too bad this can't be used for something, instead of throwing it away," she said to Bob.

"In the lab where I used to work people took it home and used it as fertilizer."

"What kind of fertilizer?"

"Ordinary fertilizer. They put it on their plants."

"Are you kidding?"

"Would I kid you? Ask anybody. You've heard of bloodmeal, haven't you? Well, it's the same thing."

Pleased with the sense that she was salvaging something that would otherwise be wasted, Leona began to take the leftover blood home. She stored it in a big jar, which she kept in the refrigerator. Now and then, when she thought about it—regularity was for work, not for home life—she poured the blood around the base of the plants in the backyard. Soon they would begin to bloom, pink and rose and deepest maroon.

*   *   *

One Sunday morning, as Norman was reading the paper at the kitchen table, she opened the refrigerator and took out the jar of blood.

"What have you got there?" he asked.

"Fertilizer."

"That's fertilizer? It looks like blood."

"It is blood. Blood from the lab. Leftover blood."

"You're using that for fertilizer?"

"You've heard of bloodmeal, haven't you?"

"Bloodmeal isn't blood."

"It works the same way."

"What idiot told you that?"

"I'm not going to argue with you. You always win arguments, that's why you like to argue," she said and went out into the garden. She was on her knees making a small well around some pink flowers when he came out. He stood watching her for a minute.

"I can't believe this. That is really disgusting."

"I don't know what you're making such a fuss about. Other people do it. I'm not the only one."

"I don't care what other people do. Can't you buy plain ordinary fertilizer?"

"Why should I buy it when this is free? I'm economizing." She poured the blood generously into the well. He was still standing, watching her. She did not look up at him.

"Tell me, Leona, what goes on in that brain of yours when you do something like this?"

She patted the earth around the well. "I don't know. I don't know if I'm thinking about anything special. Well maybe, I guess I'm thinking that it's good that the blood soaks down into the earth and it finds the right roots and—and it's sucked up somehow—as if it were coming back up again through veins and arteries—"

"Plants don't have veins and arteries."

"I know they don't but still—"

"That's just what I mean."

"What do you mean that's what you mean?"

"The way you've been acting—"

"I haven't been acting anything."

"Why don't we live like other people?" he exploded. "Would that be such a terrible thing to do? Why can't we invite other people to our house? Why can't we have a party the way other people have?"

"But you never said you wanted to give a party."

"It's not what I want to do, it's what you have to do if you want to get ahead. You have to invite the right people to your house—the important people—"

"You never told me—"

"I'm telling you now."

"All right. Okay. I'll invite whoever you want. Just tell me when, so I can get the house ready."

He seemed mollified. He turned to go back into the house.

"But I still don't see," she said suddenly, quietly, "what

inviting other people has to do with my using the blood for fertilizer."

He went back into the house, he went into the bedroom, he shut the door. He would not come out, even for lunch.

She said to the kids, Your father isn't feeling well so don't make too much noise.

Late in the afternoon she went to the bedroom to try to talk to him. As she opened the door, she saw him lying on the bed, one forearm flung over his forehead. He looked inert, as if he were paralyzed. It frightened her to see him so. What was going to happen? What should she do?

She heard a great yelling, she heard the dog barking, she ran into the family room. "What's the matter?" she asked. Natalie and Zack and Mike were on their knees in front of the guinea pigs' cage.

"They've just had babies, fifteen babies," Zack said.

"They're so ugly," said Mike.

"They're not, they're cute," said Natalie.

"Fifteen?" Leona looked into the cage. She saw the crawling mass of hairless, blind creatures.

"I can't stand it," she blew up. "I can't stand all this multiplying. It's got to stop. How can we afford to feed so many animals? You'll have to get rid of them."

"But Mom—" said Zack.

"I want you to take them to the pet store tomorrow."

"But Mom, it's not fair, you said I could have guinea pigs."

"You have the cat."

"Felicity's not mine. She's everybody's. Please, Mom, I want to keep them. I don't want to take them to the pet shop."

"Sometimes you have to do what you don't want to do," she said.

27

Leona looked around the living room once again. Everything was spotless, nothing out of place: The rugs and the white couch were clean, the black tables gleaming with polish. And outside in the garden, she could see them through the floor-to-ceiling windows, were the flowers in full bloom, shining as if they had taken the blood directly to their centers.

The sound of the doorbell startled her. Not yet, I'm not ready yet. I want it to be like this a moment longer, everything perfect, nothing used up. On the dining room table were the glass bowl and cups she had borrowed from the liquor store. She could see the cucumber slices, pale green with dark green rinds, floating like small islands in the amber punch, a lovely mixture of fruit juice and brandy and champagne. Remembering a movie she had once seen, in which elegant people milled about in an elegant room, making witty sophisticated conversation, Leona thought, Perhaps my party will be like that.

Passing, she caught her image in the small mirror in the entrance hall. Yes, she looked nice. Her hair, her eyes. She felt suddenly light and giddy, as if—who knew what might happen? That was the promise of parties, how had she forgotten?

"Mom," Natalie insisted. "The door. Open the door."

"I'm getting it. Don't get excited." She prepared to smile as she made herself walk calmly, serenely, to open it. Standing there alone was Alice Black, a secretary from Norman's lab. She was dressed in a long tight-waisted full skirt and a white blouse, her blond hair tightly curled. Leona had met her once before at a lab party and had been intimidated by her confidence and efficiency. But tonight Leona thought, When you get right down to it, she is not really that attractive. And think of what her life must be, alone, no husband, no child. Let her have her efficiency.

"Am I early?" Alice asked.

"No, you're *just* on time." Leona smiled.

"What a beautiful white couch," said Alice, advancing into the living room. "I'd never dare to have a white couch. How do you keep it so clean?"

I dare, Leona thought, Yes, I dare. She smiled mysteriously. She didn't have to say that she had worked on it for hours to get the stains out. Yes, everything is going to be all right, she told herself.

Other guests arrived in quick succession, men from Norman's lab with their wives, the men so solid looking in their dark suits, the women so stiff in their tight-waisted full skirts, their hair so tightly curled. She wasn't sure she knew all these people's names, how could she make introductions? Surely they must know each other. She offered them punch. Where was Norman? He had said he would be home right after skating. Why was he late?

Soon everyone was standing around, drinking the punch, talking quietly, the men at one end of the room, the women at the other. The women admired the garden, they admired the black and white furniture, they admired Leona's white silk dress, very tight with slits on the sides, they admired her hair, braided high on her head with a long strand of pearls woven through it. They noticed how she matched the decor of the room, black and white.

When next the doorbell rang, Leona hurried to answer. Could it be Norman? (But why would Norman ring his own bell?) It wasn't Norman, of course, it was Ninta, wearing her long brown cape with a hood. And right behind her, coming up the path, was Ralph wearing an outrageous outfit, green sports jacket, pink plaid shirt with a bright red ascot, maroon trousers and a bright red beret.

"I'm so glad you could come," Leona said to Ninta. "Can I take your coat?"

"I'll keep it, thanks, I'm a little cool."

"Have you two met? This is Ninta—" Leona, suddenly, could not remember Ninta's last name, so she hurried on, "She's a wonderful dance teacher. And this is Ralph Herbert, the director, he's just had a production at the Community Theater."

"Happy to meet any other artist in the community," said Ralph. "Not that many around. We should keep in touch. Have you heard about my new theater? I envision it as an integral part of the life of the community and—"

"I think I did read about it in the paper."

"Can I get you some punch?" asked Leona.

"Not for me, thanks," said Ninta.

"Sure, I'll have some," said Ralph.

As Leona got to the punch bowl, Natalie hissed at her from the kitchen. "Mom, come here."

"What's the matter?"

"I need help. Are the cheese puffs done yet? I can't tell," Natalie said, opening the oven door.

"I don't think so. I'd say two minutes more. Be careful when you take them out. Use that hot pad."

Returning to Ralph and Ninta with the glass of punch in her hand, Leona heard him say, "I think of the performer not as something separate, something special, but as part of the whole. Our job is to lead the audience, to help them to feel what we feel. But we're also following them, picking up what they feel, being energized by them, letting them lead us. When you think about it is all very—" he groped for a word.

"Simple," said Leona, handing him the glass.

"Yes, simple."

"I can agree with you only in part," said Ninta. "Certainly in the past it's been very important, that interaction, as you describe it. But I think one has to be very careful in these times not to relinquish one's autonomy, not to rely too much on the audience as guide. It is a grave error, I believe, for any artist in our time to keep one's eyes too intently on the audience, to try to see with their eyes, to always be thinking of what they want. The performer has to keep focusing on one thing and one thing only, where the work leads. That's the crucial—"

"When you get right down to it—" Ralph interrupted, "there's really no distinction between the audience and the performers. We're all part of the same big picture. We up there on stage are no different from those down in the audience. We have gone up on the stage for a little bit, but then it will be our turn to come back down and for them to go up. We're all artists, we're all actors, we're all dancers, we're all part of the shifting drama of life," he said huskily and finished off his punch.

Why are they carrying on like this? Leona wondered. This is not witty, this is not sophisticated. I should never have invited them. I thought they would help to liven things up, but they are neither lively nor charming. At least I thought they'd amuse each other.

"Excuse me," said Leona and started back to the kitchen.

The men from the lab were still on one side of the room, talking about their work, and the women were still on the other, talking about their children. If I set out the food, Leona wondered, will they start to mix? But where is Norman? It is getting so late. What could have happened, is he all right? What will people think if he's not here?

In the kitchen she busied herself, helping Natalie arrange the food on round plastic trays, the cheese puffs on one, little hot dogs on sticks on another, potato chips and a dip made of sour cream and dried onion soup on the other. Some of the cheese puffs were a little burned at the edges so she threw them out.

"You'd better make some more cheese puffs," she told Natalie.

"But we're out of cheese."

"How can we be out of cheese? I had another package."

"You look. I can't find any."

"I know it was here." Leona opened the refrigerator and looked on all the shelves, even through the vegetable bin with its month-old celery and its limp carrots, but she did not find the cheese.

"What's the matter? Can I help?" It was Anna, once more looking so steady and so sure, behind her.

"I've just run out of cheese. I can't understand it. I know I had another package."

"Did you look in the back, behind that big bottle?"

Leona looked, and there was the cheese, wedged behind the bottle. "I don't remember putting it there," Leona said with embarrassment. "Sometimes I think things just travel by themselves from one place to the other in the refrigerator, when you're not looking."

Anna laughed. "What's in that jar?"

Leona didn't feel like telling Anna (steady Anna, sure Anna). "Tomato juice," she answered.

"It's such a dark red for tomato juice."

"It's a new brand from the Co-op. Natalie, will you start making up some more cheese puffs right away, while I put the food on the table?"

"Can I do something?" Anna asked.

"No thanks, Natalie is giving me all the help I need. Why don't you go on in with the others and enjoy yourself?"

"You're sure? I'd be glad to help."

"I'm sure."

"Did your father call?" Leona whispered to Natalie, after Anna left the kitchen.

Natalie shook her head.

"I'm beginning to worry about him. Maybe I should call the ice rink. He couldn't have forgotten about the party, could he have?"

She heard a commotion, Ralph's deep voice raised, and she hurried into the living room and saw that he was now in the midst of the men from the lab. His beret had slipped forward over one eye. Don't let him ruin my party, please don't let him ruin my party, she prayed.

As she came up to the men she heard Gregg say with some irritation, "That's just one of those nutty ideas from science fiction. Computers are not going to take over the world. All the computer is going to do is take over certain jobs that human beings shouldn't have to do. Right after the war I worked in an aircraft plant, setting up stress calculations. It took a whole huge room with eighty women, each one on a Marchant calculator, working eight hours a day, and still they couldn't give us the answers we needed. Now that whole roomful of women has been replaced by one machine that does all they could do and much more."

"The food's on the table," said Leona softly. "Please help yourself."

"What about the women who were replaced?" asked Ralph, sharply. "What happens to them? Where will they go?"

"The food is on the table," Leona tried again.

"They'll go on to something more useful, something more creative, more human. Read *The Human Use of Human Beings*. People don't have to be drudges any more. People attack the computer when they don't even know what the hell they're talking about."

Leona hurried to the table and picked up a tray of cheese puffs. When she returned, Al Cornog, the lab manager, a tall bald man with a forbidding presence, had joined the group. "You can look at it in another way," he was saying. "The problems that we face in the world now are so vast in terms of analysis and prediction that we can't think any more in the old terms of single questions and single answers. Instead there's a range of probabilities that we have to look at. The computer's time has come because it's the necessary machine for dealing with a probabilistic world."

"Just a minute," interrupted Ralph. "Are you saying there is nothing certain in the world? Are you saying there is no such thing as an underlying structure, an underlying order?"

"That's a naive question," Al Cornog said curtly.

"There are a lot of people that consider it important."

"That's their problem." Al Cornog shrugged and walked away.

"Would anyone like to have some cheese puffs?" Leona asked.

"No, I don't want any cheese puffs. I want to ask this man something," Ralph said, pointing to Gregg. "Do you think that machines think?"

"It depends on what you mean by think. Do you mean

to work on a problem or do you mean to state or apply a conclusion? Or do you mean just to believe or suppose something? Or maybe just to be in a certain frame of mind. Thinking can mean a lot of different things. A computer thinks in a certain sense and in other ways it doesn't. It does manipulate symbols and solve problems in a way that simulates one way we think we think. But if we knew how we thought, we could program the computer to imitate us, assuming of course that it had sufficient memory."

"Can the computer create great works of art—like Shakespeare?"

"I didn't say it could."

"You're trying to reduce human beings by bringing them down to the level of a goddam machine."

"You're not listening to what I'm saying."

"The trouble with people of your ilk—"

"Ilk?" said Gregg scornfully.

"Guys like you feel you've got to control everything, you've even got to eliminate the mystery in life."

Gregg frowned. "I get sick and tired of hearing people make accusations when they don't know what they're talking about. Ask anyone who's worked with computers for a while and they'll tell you there's as much mystery in the computer as in anything else you can name. Our new machine has already reached such a state of complexity that it's impossible for anyone to know what's going on at every point, at any given moment—"

"You call that mystery? That's not what I call mystery. Mystery is—"

Gregg shrugged and walked away.

"These guys always take off when you got them cornered. Got any more punch?" he asked Leona.

"In the punch bowl, please help yourself."

Why is he being so belligerent? Leona wondered. Was he that way in the theater and I never noticed it? It's so embarrassing—Just then she saw Norman. Thank God. He was finally here. He must have come in when she wasn't looking. He was talking to Alice. Leona waved to him but he did not see her. She could tell by the way that he was gesturing that he was talking about his favorite subject, or at least his favorite subject at parties, the melting of the polar ice cap, and its consequences in the future, how cities would be flooded, how whole parts of the continent would end up under water. He seemed to take a special pleasure in such gloomy prediction. Let him talk that way, at least he's here.

In a corner she saw Gregg, looking angry, talking to Anna. He was shaking his head, No, No. From across the room she heard a commotion, Ralph's voice booming out again. (Oh please, no more arguments about thinking, I don't know if I can stand it.) She hurried over to see Ralph and Ninta facing each other, squared off like antagonists, surrounded by a group of women.

"Didn't it get to you right here in the gut when you saw them dance?"

"That's not quite the way I responded to it."

"Come on. Sure you did. It's basic human nature to respond that way."

"That doesn't happen to be my idea of either basic or natural. I thought it was theater performed with great energy and style, but it was hardly natural. It was ritual taken entirely out of context."

"Context or no context, what's the difference? The movement's the same."

"Not to me."

"Why not? Didn't you like it because it was popular, because the entire audience was responding at a gut level? It was that pulse that did it. There was no getting away from it. When you heard the beat and you saw the way those dancers' feet hit the ground—Boom! Boom!" Ralph stamped on the floor with his right foot and his whole body shook in response. "We all have that in our feet, built right in, only they're stuck in shoes that shut us off from feeling the ground. Look at those shoes you women are wearing," he gestured around the group.

The women looked at their high-heeled shoes with sharply pointed toes.

"What do those shoes have to do with the shape of anyone's feet?"

"I agree with you on that," Ninta said with asperity. She was wearing soft ballet slippers. "But that's not what we're talking about."

"What are we talking about? Aren't we talking about what people need, about contact with what's fundamental?"

"How do we know what's fundamental? We don't know anymore."

"What do you mean, how do we know? It's part of us, inside of us, that's how we know. The fundamental has always been the same going all the way back into history, and it's always going to be the same. Death, life, destruction, creation," he burst out, emphasizing each word with a chop of his hand.

For a moment Ninta was silent, she looked at the floor. Then she raised her head. She began slowly, but the more she spoke the more rapidly, even feverishly, she went on. "Don't you see that if we try to imitate a primitive form at this stage of human existence, we have to fail? It's not our form any longer. Our consciousness has gone beyond that level. What we have to do is to search for new forms appropriate to this time and place. We have to be willing to be open to these new forms, to allow them their own course of development. We have to surrender that obsession with the me-me-mine of the personal ego. That personal ego has been valuable in that it's brought us to our present level. But now we have to give it up in order to go to the next level."

"Uh-huh," said Ralph mildly, narrowing his eyes. "And how are we going to get to that next level?"

"Through discipline, detachment, objectification."

Ralph rolled his eyes. "Fat chance."

Ninta flushed. "I make no claim to originality in this. These are not my ideas alone. I have learned from other people, artists with vision, who believe that we are going to have to do this, otherwise—"

"I'll tell you something, Miss—Miss— It's never going to happen. It can't happen. You know why? Because we're never going to get rid of that ego. More than that, we don't want to get rid of that ego. We want to be what we are, human beings with desires. We want to eat, we want to drink, we want to love, we want to hate, we want to sleep, we want to fuck—"

He held up the glass of punch in his hand. "Empty," he said petulantly and lurched off to the punch bowl.

"Actually," said Ninta, "I think I'd better be going. I have to be up very early to do some work in the studio."

"I hope you're not offended," Leona whispered as she accompanied Ninta to the door. "I should have stopped him, I shouldn't have let him go on that way."

"It's very hard to stop somebody like that whose mind is shut to anything new. You didn't hear him when he was going on and on about 'Identification.' It was all false what he was saying. Everything was false."

"He was just drunk," Leona said.

"I know I shouldn't get into that kind of argument, only I don't seem to be able to help myself. When someone talks so flippantly about what I've spent my life on—"

"Thank you so much for coming," Leona said in a small voice and watched her go down the path to the sidewalk, seeing the solid mass of her brown cape disappear in the shadows of the street trees. (Poor woman—alone—)

*   *   *

She lingered at the open door. A street lamp was shining across the way, casting a pool of soft yellow light on
the pavement. Some of the houses were already dark,
enclosing those who were sleeping. Only her house was
alive with noise and with people and with music, now
that the dancing was starting. It made her feel nostalgic
for an elegant life she'd never had. She didn't feel like
going back inside, she just wanted to stay outside and
listen in the darkness, standing in front of the dark lawn,
patchy in the daytime but at night velvety smooth. (And
in the back garden the flowers were blooming red and
pink and orange.)

"What are you doing outside?" she heard someone say
and laugh on a small breath. It was Aleida in a tight-
waisted black skirt and a white frilly blouse. Her hair was
stylishly short, bleached, tightly curled. She looked so un-
like the Aleida of the dance class and the Community
Theater that Leona hardly recognized her.

"I was—I was getting a breath of air. It's so warm inside. Come in. I'm so glad you could come. Your hair
looks nice."

Then she herself laughed, oddly. How it was once again
with Aleida, how uncomfortable she was with her, as if
just being near her set up some strange confusion in her
own body, about her own body, that she was not herself
with her, that something in her was flying back and forth
when Aleida was around, would not settle down. Yet she
could force herself, had forced herself before to do what
needed to be done.

"Where's Ken?" she asked, in what seemed to be just
the right easy tone, the hostess asking her guest, as she
led her inside.

"He had to work."

"I'm so glad you came." (She already had said that.) "It's a very nice party." (Was that the right thing for her to have said?) She opened the door. "Can I get you some punch? It's a very good punch."

"I'll help myself," said Aleida.

In the living room someone tapped Leona on the shoulder. It was Al Cornog. "Let's dance."

"I'm not much of a dancer."

"I don't believe that." He took her by the hand and led her into the family room. The last record on the stack was dropping, "Bewitched, Bothered, and Bewildered."

Al held Leona very close, then spun her out, then pulled her back in expertly. "I knew you were a good dancer. I heard that you were the star in that show at the Community Theater."

"Not the star, really. There wasn't any star."

"You don't need to be modest with me."

When the music stopped, Al went to get some punch. She took off the old stack of records and put a new one on the machine. Al came back and handed her a glass of punch and she gulped it down. She had not realized how thirsty she was. She moved the black lever and the first Sinatra record dropped. It was "Night and Day."

Al took her hand and pulled her close to him. "You know," he said, breathing on her hair. "You look a lot like Elizabeth Taylor."

Of course, it was a silly thing for him to say, one of the things men said when they were trying to flatter you. "But my eyes aren't violet," she said and laughed.

Over his shoulder she saw Norman dancing with Alice. He was feverishly guiding her in his usual two-step. She knew how that felt. One—two, one—two. She laughed again, falling into the spinning around of the music, into being spun around. She could let go—almost—soon. She had begun the party for Norman, now it had to make its own life.

Only one thing more. I still have to do something, to say something to Al Cornog to let him know that I am the kind of wife who could be a help to a man who could be made an administrator.

The old record ended and a new one slipped into place.

"How is the new machine?" she asked, as he began to spin her in larger and deeper circles.

"The new machine? What do you want to know about that for?"

"It's just that I am very interested in—in—"

"When the deep—" came the soft, insistent, velvet words. The words, "random access" came into her mind as if she had been prompted. "Tell me—" she said, tripping slightly over his foot but he righted her immediately.

"Anything."

"Tell me something about random access."

He laughed and pulled her closer. "If you're interested in random access, you ought to talk to your husband. He's the expert on it."

"Of course I know that," she giggled, "but I wanted to hear what you have to say about it."

He started to answer, he got caught up in answering, he stopped dancing, he raised his voice, he kept going on and on, it seemed like hours. "It makes an enormous difference ... to be able to go directly to the data involved ... talking about a matrix, of course ... before this, when we wanted to call up data, we had to go sequentially on the tape, but this way—"

She was listening, she was trying hard to listen but she was irretrievably lost. She wanted to sit down, to lie down, she was sick of listening. But she kept nodding and saying, "Really? Is that right?"

"Round and round—" She heard the words spinning. (Am I going to be sick? I never should have had that punch. I know I can't drink.) Stillness was what she wanted, to be away from this noise, from all these bodies moving, from these words that had no meaning.

"Thank you very much for the lovely dance and the lovely discussion but I'm afraid I must leave you to attend to my guests."

She slipped through the milling others but in the doorway bumped into Anna, who was just coming in to dance with Gregg. She went out to the kitchen. Where was Natalie? She should be making the coffee by now, she'd told her around midnight she should put the coffee on.

She made her way down the hallway to Natalie's room. The door was shut. Don't tell me she's gone to sleep already, when I need her help with the coffee and the cakes. She pushed the door open.

"Natalie—" In the dim night light she saw a body—no, two bodies embracing. Not Natalie. Not Natalie. A woman in black and white, with short light hair. Aleida. A man. Norman. Am I dreaming? Am I drunk?

Leona closed the door. I don't believe it. Yet in a moment it was the only thing she had ever believed.

She leaned against the doorjamb, hearing the sounds of music and laughter, harsh sounds, not elegant. She did not know what way to move, she was not even sure she knew what moving was. Yet something put one foot in front of another and got her to the bedroom, sat her on the edge of the bed, piled high with the guests' coats. She sat and stared, still seeing what she did not want to see. Shivering, she pulled the top coat out to wrap around her.

"Who took my cover?" a voice boomed out.

It was Ralph huddled among the coats. He raised himself up partway and groaned. "Oh, it's you."

He fell back among the coats. "The room won't stop spinning. That punch of yours, what was in it?"

He had asked her a question. She had heard his words, they required an answer. "I don't know . . ."

"You made it, goddammit, you have to know what you put in it."

"What I put in it," she said vaguely. "Brandy and champagne and some apple juice and soda and cucumbers. Oh, what do I care?"

"You don't care. You give your guests a punch that's poison and you don't care?"

"I got it from a recipe book. I followed the recipe exactly."

"I have never felt worse in my life. I have thrown up twice and it didn't help."

"Maybe it wasn't the punch. Maybe you've got a stomach flu or an allergy."

"You may be right. Maybe it was the cucumbers. Cucumbers are very hard on my stomach. I know I shouldn't eat cucumbers. But I didn't think it was the same drinking cucumbers." He groaned again.

"Do you want an aspirin?"

"No aspirin. I just want this to be over. I—"

He jumped up and ran into the bathroom. She heard him puking—in the toilet, she hoped.

When he came out he said, "Finally. I guess I got rid of it all. I do feel better. Finally." He touched his head with his right hand. "Where's my beret? I'll bet one of those computer assholes stole my beret. Those jerks. They've got computers for brains. That's why they think computers think. What do they know about life? About feeling? What do they know about how human beings feel? The human use of human beings—my ass. Ah, there's my beret." He picked it up from the floor and put it on his head. He looked in the mirror over the dresser and adjusted it to a more rakish angle. "Ralph Herbert, director of the New Theater, the one man with a vision in the land of small-brained men, who know only two alternatives: one—zero, on—off."

He turned and came over to Leona. She was bent over, her head down, her hands wrapped over her belly, rocking back and forth. His hand shot out and seized her wrist. "Say, I saw you dancing in there. Pretty sexy. How come you didn't do that in my show instead of kicking that tree wrong way around?"

"I didn't kick the tree. I fixed it. I turned it back around the way I was supposed to. I was the one who danced 'The Dance of the Mother,' " she wailed.

"Okay, okay. Don't get so excited. You know how it is when you do one show after another. You get a little confused. I'm entitled."

He yawned and stretched, then wet his lips with his tongue, "God, I'm so thirsty. Do you have anything else cold to drink around here—something beside that punch?"

"In the refrigerator. Please, help yourself. Please, go."

"I'm going. I don't need a second invitation."

She lay down on the bed and closed her eyes. The hole, the great hole of belief was still there. She sat up. He was gone. She looked at the coats. Other people's coats on my bed—Norman's and my bed—other people's coats, other people's bodies.

She got up and opened the glass door to the patio. She stepped outside. She closed the door behind her. She went over to the bed of flowers. She knelt down and touched the leaves, so alive, flamingly alive, so bound to the earth, their roots so deep and grasping. She pulled at the edge of a blossom. Did flowers cry when they were pulled out, the cry of lives uprooted? A sound came to her of her own wrenched weeping, that was overcome shortly by the harshness of another sound—loud, sharp, abrupt—from inside the house. She jumped up—she who never jumped—and ran—she who never ran—through the open patio door to the living room, through the living room (where Natalie was sleeping on the white couch) into the kitchen where the others were standing around looking in horror at Ralph who was spitting red into the sink. In his hand was a glass of red liquid, from the jar in the refrigerator.

28

When Aleida came home from the party, Ken was just where he had been when she left. He was sitting on the redwood bench, the cards on the table in front of him. He was playing solitaire. At a distance from him, out of the house, she'd been able to think of him as shapeless, inert, his charm—whatever that was—having vanished. Now that he was here in the flesh before her, she saw that he was heavy, dense, a burden.

He didn't say anything to her. He was waiting for some word, some gesture from her. An apology for going and leaving him alone? When he was the one who had refused to go, refused even to give a reason? When he was the one who'd said, If you want to go, go?

He'd get no apology from her.

She went to the bathroom, she got ready for bed. She got into bed. Lying there, unable to sleep, she heard the slap-slap-slap of the cards on the wooden table. It was like an order: Say something, say something, say something.

She got up and shut the bedroom door. The sound came through the flimsy wood. It was up to her to block it out, to block him out. She would make her mind a blank by sheer effort.

But there was this dangerous thing that began to happen to her. She began to feel herself becoming muddier around the edges (becoming even more approximate), as if she extended out for miles, as if she couldn't be contained within her own skin, or as if, inversely, she were withdrawing to a small point that, with the least bad luck, might simply disappear.

She threw the blanket off. She heard the slap-slap-slap, a sound become tyrannical, insisting attention be paid to it and it only. Nothing ever existed before this. Nothing ever existed after this. There is only this sound, this hole of sound, to be pulled down into.

She got up, she went into the living room. The TV was on but the volume was turned way down.

"How can you hear it?" she said.

"I'm not listening."

She walked over and pushed the knob in. The picture shrank to a flat grayness.

"Leave it alone," he said. She pulled the knob out. Figures moved, turned—

Now if she could just get out, go out, move—but she was trapped in here.

She went into the bedroom, she lay down. It surrounded her, the slap-slap-slap. She got up. She went into the living room. She looked, she had to look at this being, this one who was sitting on the bench, this being whom she once thought was the shining center of the earth, and now was—pudgy.

She sat in the Morris chair—the cracked and peeling

Morris chair. She watched him place the cards on the table, three by three, examining the cards already laid out. She could tell he was stuck. He had not won. (Loser, loser.)

He picked up the cards. He shuffled. She watched him deal them onto the table, the first row face down, the last row face up. She saw his hands, she felt his hands, as if she were doing the dealing.

Someone had to make a different move, he or she. Which would it be? She knew he was waiting for her to go first. She would wait him out. She could feel that in him, that uneasiness at waiting. She could bear that better than he.

He got up. He threw the cards down. She shut her eyes. She heard him move. She waited. (Something like desire stirred in her. It had come out and looked and was now waiting.) She heard him go past her. She opened her eyes. He was sitting on the couch. He was looking at her. Suddenly he lay down on the couch.

She got up. She went over to the couch. She sat on the floor beside him. He put out his hand. He touched her hair. "I liked your hair long."

"I wanted a change."

"You look like a boy, a cute boy."

He began to tell her a story about his friend Scotty, when they were in the Marines, in the Pacific, about how Scotty had picked up a native girl on one of the islands, how he had bought her a drink and got her to go with him to a room, how the girl, suddenly terrified said to him, But I'm a boy, and Scotty said, But he was so pretty and so sweet I went ahead and took him anyhow.

He laughed and sat up. He lit a cigarette. He smiled— charmingly. He asked her about the party.

She told him who was there. She told him about Ralph and the blood. He said, What the hell was a bottle of blood doing in the refrigerator? And he laughed again.

The easy sound of his laughter reminded her that she had gone down with him into that hole and now he had come back, was coming back, but she was still in it, still climbing out, while he was acting as if nothing had happened.

Why do I have to do this? she raged. Other women don't have to do this. Other women are luckier—more beautiful, taller, slimmer.

Once again, she could not help herself, she said to him what she knew she should not say. Words came rushing out, as if what had been dammed would no longer be pent up, as if they had a life of their own that had to be heard, as if she had no choice, as if otherwise she would never again have relief or release, as if it were the very urge to motion itself that must be satisfied.

So let him go back into that hole, she thought.

"How do you think we're going to manage now that you've walked out on that job too?"

He looked at her with surprise. "What do you mean? You think I should have kept that fucking job? Oh no, not me. I'm not going to take that kind of shit."

"Sometimes you have to take what you don't want to take."

She saw that he was close to the edge now. But she would not, could not stop.

Out poured words about responsibility, responsibility to other people beside yourself. And then, with no space between one thought—one rage—and the next came the words, spat out: "I hate living in this hovel."

"Oh, so now we're back to that again. You're like a broken record, Aleida. You know, it wouldn't be such a hovel, if you took care of it."

"It'll always be a hovel. Nothing can change that. It's too small and it's dingy and it's too dark and—"

He got up and started out of the room. She held on to him with her words, yelling, "You said you were going to think about getting a house. What are you waiting for? When you're sixty and ready to retire? Is that what you're waiting for?"

He came back in again. He looked at her. He went out, he came back in again. He sat on the couch with the blanket thrown over it. He put his hands on his knees. He looked at the floor, not at her. "If you want to buy a house so badly, you can go and get a job to help pay for it."

"What kind of job could I get?"

"You can always go back to being a bookkeeper, the way you were before I married you."

"Back to those dead figures. No, thanks. I want something important, something different, something that makes me feel alive."

"People don't usually pay you for doing something that makes you feel alive."

He got up and went back to the table. He picked up the cards.

She went back to bed. Her body felt emptied out except for what had poured into her from him, from his inertness, as if it had been a kind of poisoned sperm. She was left with a raging need, a sense that everything around her was rotten, was ash, everything—this, that, sex, dancing, Peralta, this house, any house.

As she lay there, her body ached for something, anything but this that she had. She realized she no longer heard the slap-slap-slap. Frightened, she jumped up and ran into the now dark living room. She went over to the couch, he was sleeping, she heard his breathing. Yes he was sleeping, one of the shadows.

She went back into the bedroom, she threw herself onto the bed. She could not fall asleep but suddenly she was asleep. Awaking, she knew she had been dreaming, had heard things scurry in corners, things that had nothing to do with light and air. Suddenly, unexpectedly, it was as if a small hole opened within her, through which she herself could slip, to find herself on the other side of desire, desire in and of itself, desire leading her, and she plunging after it, being led by an image, an image that made desire deeper, an image of him, of Ken with a woman, not herself. She saw her playing with him as he liked to be played with. She saw him responding, she urged him within herself to respond, to be enticed, to give in, to be overcome. Feeling his feeling, she began to touch herself, here, there on her body, this opening, that opening, any opening. She trembled at the image of them in an embrace that she was witnessing and directing and feeling at the same time, inciting them, being incited herself, going on and on, to a higher and higher pitch till she could feel herself object and subject, nothing but pleasure—pleasure for herself alone. She was getting there ... she was getting there ... She got there.

29

Each Tuesday at two, without fail, I went to Ninta's class. Leona never came. (Someone said that Leona had gone away.) Aleida came sporadically but she seemed detached. She went through the movements in a desultory way and always left before the class was over.

Week by week the other women began to drop out, one by one.

Ninta herself seemed to be getting thinner, more angular, sharper, as if she were being consumed by her own intensity. Now, when she leaped, her motion had the odd effect of disembodiment. I felt I was seeing a creature without blood, without sweat—but all tension—as if she were metal fired, drawn out to the finest wire.

Fervently Ninta said, and just as fervently I wanted to believe her, that technique was a training imposed upon the body that it must submit to, but finally, paradoxically, through that submission, it would be loosed into freedom. I began to see that what was being presented to me as an example to be followed was a vision of an ideal body, an ideal motion, an ideal art.

But I myself felt rooted in a body that went this way and that way, that discounted what I thought most important, that suddenly rebelled and refused, that seemed to have its own hidden intentions—No, I would not think again of how I had kicked the tree during the performance—No, I had not deliberately kicked the tree—But if resolve could achieve anything, I was resolved, at least while I was in this hall, in this class, to overcome what was working against me.

Even if it meant a perpetual fight against some ultimate condemnation in myself—a condemnation that told me that I was not good enough, not ideal enough, I would persist—even though my body reinforced this judgment, slyly anticipating and forestalling what I tried to do, tightening my shoulder joints, tightening my hip joints, tightening my tendons and my muscles. If it was necessary to fight my own body, then I would have to do that. (But how does one fight one's own body, isn't one's own body one's self?)

I was puzzled and elated at the same time, I found myself leaping higher than ever, but in the midst of leaping would come the realization of a return to earth even further back than where I'd started.

At times I felt as if I was a child in a perpetual game of "Giant Steps," being told to "Go back ... Go back ..."

30

One night I dreamed I was in the backseat of a car, stopped at a red light. The light turned green but the woman in the driver's seat did not start. Behind us, I heard other drivers blowing their horns. Still the woman refused to move.

Only as the light was about to change to red again did the woman start, inching along in a new refusal. Seeing a policeman on a traffic island ahead, I rolled down the window and called out to him. But he was busy talking to a woman who held a child in her arms and he paid no attention to my complaint.

I woke up feeling an intense, unreasoning resentment at the woman in the driver's seat. Unreasoning, even for a dream. I tried to recapture the woman's image exactly, or as exactly as the dream, now departing, would allow. I thought she was stolid, heavyset, with a thick short neck. But there was something else about her, something in her attitude, in her body's attitude, that had caused me to feel helpless in my anger.

I realized, now that I was awake, that there had been a smugness in her, in her absolute conviction in her own power to go slow, to refuse to hurry. That power was rooted in her history, in her past that I knew nothing about, though clearly she was familiar to me.

Nevertheless, whether I knew or didn't know her and her history, because she chose to go slow, I had had to go slow.

31

One Tuesday I arrived at the class to find only Ninta in the hall. There were no other students but myself.

"Isn't there going to be a class today?" I asked.

"Yes, there's supposed to be a class but—" Ninta gestured aimlessly with her hands. "Perhaps people were held up ... Though you would think they would have called me. But no one called ... We'll wait a few moments and see."

As I waited, I began to go through a series of stretches on the floor. Now and then I would look up and see

Ninta. She kept walking back and forth. She kept looking at the door. She was not looking at me.

The minutes went by, ten, fifteen, and still no one came. "It looks as if you're the class today," Ninta said, smiling and not smiling.

I didn't know what to say to her. I thought I should say something—give an explanation, an apology for the others—but the chance to speak had already passed.

Ninta took her place in front of me, her back to the stage. We began as we always began the class, with slow relaxations and stretches, each movement connected to the next, progressing to ever more demanding sequences.

There was, I realized, even as I was trying to give full attention to the movements, a slight panic within me. It was as if being here with Ninta alone, facing her alone, being watched by her, alone, was too hard for me to deal with. As if the situation allowed me no escape, no place to hide. As if I was not ready—as if I needed time—as if I needed the presence of the others in the class—as if I needed anonymity.

Ninta kept watching me intently, focusing on every motion I made. She kept correcting me, she kept urging me to let go, saying, Can't you feel how when you move into a contraction, you must release the tension in the back? Can't you see how the motion has to keep flowing?

She suggested that I try an improvisation on a turn in the form of a figure eight. I forced myself to move, to turn. I turned to the left and then to the right. I did a fast turn and then a slow one. I changed levels from a high turn to a low one and then back to a high turn again. Even as I did it, I realized it was planned, thought out, stilted in its execution.

Ninta said, "I have the sense that your body starts the movement and then stops, starts again and then stops, as if it were constantly being interrupted, as if your concentration gets going and then there's a distraction and your concentration breaks and you have to start all over. Whatever the interruption is, whatever thought or feeling, see if you can incorporate it into the movement as part of the continuing impulse."

I tried once more. Almost as soon as I began, I could feel the fading of the impulse within me. I felt the sense of my own inadequacy to do what I was asked to do. I tried to force myself to go on. I thought, Others—what others?—keep going without any worry or self-reproach. Why can't I? What is stopping me?

I felt anxiety—boredom—I felt I shouldn't have come. I felt I was repeating, repeating, going nowhere. At the same time, some strange, almost feverish excitement, was pushing me on (Because I was being watched? Because I was the only one being watched?)

"No," said Ninta. "It's still not flowing. It's not working. Maybe we'd better not try to approach the problem of continuity so directly. Let's try something else, a different kind of improvisation from what we've been doing. I want you to take a motion from daily life. Start out with any habitual motion, something you do without even knowing you're doing it. For example, walking from one room to another. When you do that in your ordinary life you move with a purpose, an intention. Maybe you're taking a wastebasket from one room to another. You don't even think about the walking. It's second nature. And while you're walking maybe you notice some dust on the floor, or maybe you're thinking about a bill you need to pay or a call you have to make. See if you can do that."

When I finished, she said, "Fine, fine. But that's not dance, that's pantomime."

"Now, let's take it a step further. See now if you can strip that movement down. See if you can begin to experience the motion in isolation, as motion for its own sake. I want you to take away the particulars, the specifics. I want you to strip away the external references you were thinking about and just get to the essential quality of a walk."

Standing in place, the focus of Ninta's eyes, I felt as if I was on a stage and someone said, Move without gestures, or someone said, Speak without words. Or rather, as if I had the words and the gestures somewhere in the back of my mind (in the back of my body?) but, unable to use them, I had to plead my cause dumbly, silent. (What cause?)

Moving, I stumbled and caught myself. I felt stuck, as if I was trying to solve a problem with all unknowns, as if I was trying to tell a story without plot or character or place, as if I was trying to paint a landscape without line or color.

"Isolate the movement," Ninta called out. "Break it down. Let it become nothing but the placing of one foot before the other, the leaning forward into the ball of the foot, the shifting of weight in the pelvis."

I took a step, one foot, then the other foot. I felt a deadness, an ineptness in the motion. I forced myself to take another—abstracted—I was thinking and not thinking at the same time. (It was like thinking about thinking.) I felt another impulse readying itself within me, rising up—in my mind, in her body—a jerk, a spasm, that ridiculous, ugly motion that made me look like a fool, the one at which people—Aleida—people—laughed.

"No, no, no," said Ninta. "It's all muddled, it's muddy, it's flaccid, it's neither here nor there, it's weighted with irrelevant things. Don't you see?"—and now her voice was so urgent it was almost pleading—"Don't you see that once you get it stripped down, then you can start to build it up, then you can begin to exaggerate this or that, then you can do variations, then you can make it become something entirely different, new, not limited by your previous experience, but first, first, you have to isolate it—"

She stopped suddenly. "I know how hard this is. I struggled for it for years. You mustn't be discouraged if it doesn't come. It will come. I know that. I tell you it will come. And when it comes, then your work will be entirely different. The way you move will be entirely different. You'll be able to go on to—to things you never expected."

I sighed and shook my head. "It doesn't feel like it. It feels as if it will never change."

"It will," she said.

After a moment she said, "Do you want to try another improvisation? There's still time left."

"Could we instead—could you—Would you be willing to show me some of your own work, one of your own dances?"

"You want to see one of my dances?" She laughed in some surprise. "But I don't perform any more, I just don't."

"Just this once, couldn't you?"

"But—" she said. Then she shrugged. "Yes. All right. Why not? Since you're the only one here today. Why not? I'll show you a short piece of mine, one I did many years ago. When I used to perform. In my other life."

She walked out to the center of the hall. "It begins on the ground," she said.

She placed herself on the floor, her body in the black leotard making a strange convoluted shape. Slowly, almost imperceptibly, she began to move, so slowly that for a moment I had the sense that it was not Ninta, not even a body, but some organism evolving, slowly, bit by bit, the continuity never broken, the movement becoming a twisting that turned back on itself, going inside itself, then coming out again. The movement went on

116

and on, so slowly, yet so intently, it was drawing out time, extending time . . .

It proceeded, that motion—I don't know how long it took—till finally it—she—it had risen to a standing position, a strange posture, the weight on one leg, the upper body leaning over, arms extended out . . .

But now happened what I had not expected. A sense of disorder, of grotesqueness, entered into me. As if through my eyes, through watching this being who was Ninta—but not Ninta—I had become a part of what she was creating. I was no longer observer, but participant, part of this evolution in motion that was even now creating a sense of strangeness so pervasive that the hall itself began to alter, became deeper, darker, filled with shadows.

The head moved from side to side, the arms extended further, all this in slowness, but with a tension so great it was as if a spasm had been drawn out, begun and continued, an anarchic thing (though in full control) extending out beyond its own shape into terror, pity, awe, longing, going on and on, not coming to climax, but simply, suddenly, ended.

An expression of surprise or pain came over Ninta's face. "If you'll excuse me, I'll be back in a moment," she said in a strained voice and hurried out of the hall into the dressing room.

Standing, unmoving, I looked at the stage with its shabby blue curtains (closed), turned and looked at the choir loft, lifted my eyes and looked up at the lights which hung from the long poles, glaring. I recalled something my mother had said to me when I was a girl, a warning about being careful not to go too far with probing, with asking questions. You can go only so far and no further, she had said. There was a word she used. Ketz. Was that it? I remembered the gesture of my mother's hand as she cut the air with the side of her hand, as she said the word. Ketz. (Perhaps I had asked her how it was possible to explain the vengeful actions of God in the Old Testament.)

Ninta appeared in the doorway, a towel held to her nose. The towel was spotted with blood. "I can't seem to stop it," she said. "It's so strange. I never have nosebleeds."

"Don't you think you'd better lie down?"

She lay on her back on the floor, her pale face almost dead white. She held the towel to her nose. The blood flowed out in an everwidening stain. She began to tremble.

"Are you cold? Can I get your cape?"

"Please. It's in the dressing room."

I got the cape and covered Ninta but she did not stop trembling. "Do you want me to take you to a doctor?"

"No, no. It's only a nosebleed. It will stop soon."

"Once when Rebecca had a nosebleed, the doctor told me to pinch the end of her nose."

Ninta dropped the bloody towel to the floor and grasped the end of her nose between her thumb and forefinger. How sharp, how hawklike her nose was. Her head arched back, her mouth open, she lay as if gasping for breath.

Looking down at her, I thought of how she leaped, how she sprang into the air, as if she'd overcome gravity and her own earthbound body. But now she was motionless on the floor, like a wounded black bird, fallen from a great height.

"I think it's stopped." Throwing off the cape, Ninta sat up. "Yes, I think it's stopped." She shook her head. She smiled wanly. "I'm sorry to have made all this fuss. I never get nosebleeds."

"Would you like me to take you home?"

"No, I'll be fine, though probably we should end the class for today. I'm sorry, this was so stupid of me." She stood up, she looked around the hall. She started to say something then stopped. She made an aimless gesture with her hand. (Muddied. Muddled.) "You've heard—have you?—about Aleida's class?"

I shook my head. "No," I said.

"She began it some weeks ago. I just found out she's been using the hall, though she never asked me for permission. She had the key—She's taken my students. No, it's wrong to say, 'My students.' They don't belong to me. If they choose to go to her class, that's their choice. It's not as if it were a matter of betrayal. Do you know what she calls her class? 'Motion and Emotion.' That's what she calls it. She's teaching them to express their feelings in movement. What does that mean? Is she going to teach them to express joy like this?" Ninta raised her arms to the ceiling. "Or sorrow? Like this?" She clutched her arms to her breast and twisted her face into piteousness. But it was not really piteousness, as it had not really been joy.

I flinched at her gestures, I shrank away from the words that Ninta was saying. I didn't want to know what Aleida was doing or not doing. But Ninta would not or could not stop.

"She is telling the students that I am opposed to feeling in my work. It is not true. What I am opposed to is the use of dance for something other than its own sake. What she's doing is self-indulgence, showing off for the pleasure of being seen, it's a making public of what should remain internal, private—it's done for justification—for excuse—"

A trickle of blood was flowing from her nose again, red against the pale skin, dripping onto, dropping down from her lips.

"I'll get you some cold water," I said.

In the small bathroom beyond the dressing room, I ran the water and soaked some paper towels. I did not look into the small cracked mirror above the sink. When I got back to the hall, Ninta was again lying on the floor, holding the white towel to her nose with one hand. Her other arm was flung out to the side, in a twisted position.

I felt as if I was in Ninta's body and my own at the same time, as if lament was being shared, lament at all that was unjust and cruel in life, a cruelty wreaked by those who didn't give a damn, who only thought of themselves. But now this identification—if that was what it was—asked for action in the real world against those who took advantage, who manipulated, who used others for their own gain.

"I'll call a meeting of the students, all of those who have worked with you. I know that if you tell them what is going on, they'll help, they won't let this happen. I know they won't. I'll call them for you. I'll tell them—"

Ninta sat up. She said, "It stopped." She stood up. She said, "I think people must make their own decisions. If they go with her, then they go with her. That is their choice."

"But if you would talk with them or let me talk with them—"

"I must be getting home. I have so much to do—" But she did not go. She looked at the stage. She said, "I thought it was possible to start all over again here. If Ralph Herbert hadn't come—But when he came—and all of you—"

"We came back. I came back—"

"Yes, you came back," Ninta said.

I saw the towel with blood upon the floor where Ninta had left it. I thought of Leona and of the blood in the jar. (Blood had to be thought of.)

I picked up the towel.

I said, "You can get rid of the stain if you rinse it out with cold water before it sets. Shall I do it now?"

"No, I'll do it at home." Ninta held out her hand and

took the towel. Still she did not move. She clutched the towel in both hands, wringing it tighter and tighter. "I never expected this from her. I tried to teach her everything I knew. I feel—I felt—I treated her as if she was my own daughter.

I saw something tighten in Ninta's face, like a final locking, a throwing away of the key. "I feel as if—as if—she betrayed me," she said, her voice gagging.

* * *

Only later, when I was driving home, about to turn into my own street, did I realize that I had said nothing to Ninta about her dance.

32

Leona often thought of Peralta. She recalled the hills, the sun, her house, the white couch, the black lamps and tables. Here she was in a flat furnished with someone else's stuff, all looking as though it had been discarded by Goodwill. And out the window all you could see were other windows.

She thought of her garden. She longed to be there, to

feel the ground underfoot, to see the flowers, to smell the morning smells. But she had had to go. She was driven out into this world of strangers. Yes, she had Natalie with her but Natalie was neither stranger nor company with her sullenness. She should have left Natalie with him too. How were they going to live on what she was making?

She began to count and counting threw her into a frenzy. Decide, decide, she kept urging herself, even as she didn't know what she must decide, on what she should base her decisions. On hope, on fear, on trust, on practicality? What was practicality? To get a better-paying job? (Where I am now is a rotten place to work, the way they watch your every step, how long you take for a break, how long you're in the bathroom. But were other labs in the city different?) She should find another place to live. She hated this apartment with its sallow green paint and its dripping faucets and its smell of old cabbage cooking.

The image of Peralta gleamed like a heavenly city. How could she ever get back to it? One night she dialed their telephone number—the number that used to be hers too but now was only his. He answered but the moment she heard his voice, she hung up without saying a word. She thought of him, standing there, holding the receiver in his hand, putting it back in its cradle. What did he do now for food? What did he do at night? Without her he was the greatest stranger of all. Yet sometimes, awaking, alone in the cold bed at first light, she felt him so close to her she could almost reach out and touch him. She reached out. He was not there. She got up, she got dressed, she got ready to go to work. She went out the door and shut the closeness in behind her.

*   *   *

Walking in the park one warm Sunday with Natalie, Leona saw far up ahead on the path a woman coming toward them swathed in a brown cape, striding along as if nothing or no one else existed beside herself. Not wanting Ninta to see her—what would she say to her?—Leona turned aside into a grove of redwoods. She stayed looking up into the filtered light until Natalie became impatient. "Aren't we going to go? Why are we standing here?" Leona went back onto the path. The woman was just passing. It wasn't Ninta. It was somebody else wearing a brown cape in this warm weather. Leona felt deceived by her in more ways than one.

She stopped at a meadow to watch some boys playing ball. One of them reminded her of Zack. She should have let him keep the guinea pigs. Why did she make him get rid of them? I should have—I never should have—

Everywhere she looked she saw couples, couples holding hands, or walking with arms around each other. Only she was without love. She looked up at the black rocks rising beyond the lake with initials and names scrawled upon them, intertwined, and a guttural sound arose from her throat.

"What did you say?" asked Natalie.

"Nothing. What are you walking that way for? Stand up straight. And don't shuffle your feet. What will people think when they see you?"

"What people? I don't know anybody here."

"What difference does it make? Do you want them to think you're a clod? What is wrong with you? I take you to the park and all you do is complain."

"I don't like it here. It's no fun here. I wish we could go home."

"We can't."

"Why can't we?"

"We just can't."

"Why?"

"You're too young to understand."

"Why do you say that to me?" Natalie began to cry. "I am not too young to understand."

"I don't understand, myself," Leona said, helplessly.

For she did not understand why she had done what she had done. It was not as if she herself had decided. It was as if it had been ordained, not by will—whatever that was—but by something even less clear, to which there was no possibility of saying no.

*   *   *

After Ralph spat the blood into the sink, after the others had all gone home, she stayed up to clean and kept on cleaning, as if cleaning would wipe out all that had happened. To rinse the dishes and the glasses, to put them in the dishwasher, to wash the punch bowl, to throw away the last sad cucumbers, to see them vanish down the garbage disposal, to sweep, to vacuum, to straighten up, to take the dishes out of the dishwasher, to put them away, her dishes.

As she walked down the hallway to her bedroom she had felt suddenly and irrevocably, These are no longer my walls. (As if they were walls of a tomb through which she had been wandering for a long time, but now it was time to go out into the daylight.)

She had made herself go to bed, though she wasn't tired. She had gotten into bed with him, she had kept close to the edge on her side, she had not slept. The night seemed to go on and on, while she was waiting for the light. Shortly before dawn he had awakened and turned to her, half asleep. He had come over to her, he had said nothing, she had said nothing. Quickly, quickly he had entered her. She had not protested. It was as if this were a final performance on her part, a farewell performance. She had felt a certain distant tenderness toward him, a sudden strange generosity in the thought of giving in to him this one last time. No, it was not giving in. She was not really there. She was already somewhere else. She had had a sense of giving while she withheld that which was most important, that which was beyond, outside, ahead.

So she had thought, so she had felt, that night before leaving. But when she had come away to the city, leaving the boys and taking only Natalie, the thoughts, the feelings, had not held. Many times, during the day and the night, at work and in the apartment, she was overcome by regret. Inside and outside were both unfamiliar. In the streets, in the market, she did not know any faces. She was isolated in a world where you had to start from scratch and make everything up yourself, in which there were no rules. It seemed to her now that in Peralta, in her house, with her family, it was as if she had been floating on the surface of a great salt lake, that she might drift down but she would at once be buoyed up by her life with others. She did not have to hold herself up. But here, there was no one but Natalie—and what help was Natalie?—she had only herself to hold herself up. She was no longer suspended; she drifted down, she fell.

*   *   *

Each day, after work, when Leona climbed the long steep staircase to her flat, she was more winded than the day before. At the landing, she stopped to get her breath. She felt as if she'd been dragging herself uphill for too many years. It was true that she had been putting on a little weight, but not that much. I'm going to go on a diet today, she told herself, though she knew she would not. She hated the idea of counting calories, of withholding food from herself, all in the name of being thinner. It's not my nature to be thin.

She opened the door and there was Natalie, who was supposed to be doing her homework, not doing her homework. She was slumped in a chair, looking out the window to the windows across the court.

"If you don't sit up, you're going to get a double curvature in your spine and then you'll have to be in a cast."

Natalie shrugged and slumped even more. Deliberately, to spite me, Leona decided. Seeing Natalie's face so sullen and withdrawn, she felt herself being dragged down further, falling faster.

"I don't know why I brought you with me. You're nothing but a burden. And I don't need any more burdens. Do you want to go home? Do you want to go back to your father? Is that what you want? I'll pack you up and put you on the train tomorrow, if that's what you want."

Natalie muttered something under her breath.

"Stop mumbling. Speak clearly."

"I said that isn't what I want," said Natalie, her voice wavering.

Leona took a deep breath and sighed. The promise of Natalie's tears consoled her. "All right then, but act cheerful for God's sake."

"I don't feel cheerful."

"Then pretend. It won't hurt you to pretend. And if you pretend enough, who knows, you might feel more cheerful."

*   *   *

To be fair, she knew it was not only Natalie who was pulling her down. For there was something else that was happening to her, something in her own body that made it seem remote, as if it were being turned aside, or turning in, or turning away. She felt it first one day when she was lying down, then she had felt it when she was standing, now she even felt it when she was walking, this pulling down in her belly that was also like a streaming in or a deep trembling. She didn't know what it was, she didn't have any word for it. It would go away and she would forget about it, and then it would come back again stronger. Maybe I have a growth, she thought, terrified, and then she thought, At least that would end things and I could stop having to hold myself up. But no, she didn't mean that, she didn't want to die. Maybe it is nerves, maybe this is what people call nerves, maybe it will all go away.

But it not only didn't go away, it came back more often and stronger. She felt that she'd taken up residence in a foreign body, a body that was vengefully strange and unyielding.

She made an appointment at a clinic. The doctor, a soft-spoken middle-aged man, listened noncommittally when she told him about her symptoms, about the streaming and the trembling. He told her to get undressed so that he could examine her. She didn't much care for the undressing, she didn't like having to lie down and put her feet in the stirrups, but she did as the nurse told her. The doctor came in, he bent down, he looked, he poked around. Leona stared at the ceiling above her.

"A growth? Sure you have a growth." He laughed. "You're pregnant," he said.

"But it can't be. I've been having my periods all along."

"Full periods?"

"Maybe a little less bleeding but—"

"It can happen."

"But when—how long?"

"I'd say you're at least three months now."

"Three months?"

It was almost exactly three months since that night.

*　*　*

As she climbed the long staircase to her flat, her own feebleness enraged her. She wanted to cry out, It is unfair, that this happened to me. Now when I have finally set myself free, gone out into the world, now I am caught again, and it is even worse than before. I am caught and I have no one to help me. No one but Natalie. And she is no help.

On the landing she stopped and drew her breath. If she could have, at that moment, she would have stopped giving breath that was life to what was within her, but of course she could not stop breathing. Breath came of its own, in and out, no matter what you did, it came, it was natural for it to come. I must accept it—this growth, this being—as I have accepted things all my life. I accepted and accepted until three months ago and then when I left I thought I was through with accepting. But now I have to accept this. Now there will be a different end to what he did, what she did, what I felt, what I saw, what I did.

*　*　*

I made myself go to bed. I wasn't tired, yet I went to our bed. (I could have slept on the couch. Why didn't I sleep on the couch?) Norman was already asleep. I didn't know if he knew about Ralph and the blood, if he had heard Ralph roar, "What the hell—blood in the refrigerator? Is there some goddammed vampire in the house?"

There was a vampire in the house, sucking out its life. From my side of the bed, far away from his sleeping body, I felt it between us. I saw it smiling, I saw it laughing, I saw it turning and touching him. He woke up, he turned, he threw himself on it. No, I can't, I won't look.

I looked. I saw them together. I saw and heard them together. Jealousy was sucking at me, making me look. I looked, I saw it was all his fault. I felt, No, it is not his fault, it is her fault. She seduced him, she did it all. She is the powerful one. He's being directed by her just as I was. What I thought was my moving was never my moving. He turned, he moved over, he touched me. No, I thought, No. I will get out of bed, I will. I did not get out of bed. I did not push him away.

And now I am being punished for what I didn't do, by being forced to bear this—memory alive.

Don't remember. How? An abortion? Where or how could I get one? I have no money and even if I had the money, how would I find someone to do it? She remembered her girlhood friend Mary Pelfini and how she had almost died on the kitchen table of a dirty butcher. (I don't want to die.) Mary Pelfini had ended up in the hospital with blood poisoning. And then, when she was finally better, when she came home, that very same day, that very same boy who had gotten her pregnant in the first place came to her again and she had slept with him without any protection—again. How could she have?

How could you have? she asked herself.

*   *   *

In the morning Leona awoke with a high fever. She went to the doctor. "Why didn't you come back before this?" He shook his head. "Didn't you see how bloated and puffy you are? Your condition is dangerous. You're going to have to stay in bed and take this medication and if the fever doesn't go down in a couple of days, you'll have to go to the hospital."

Couldn't she let it die? she wanted to ask. Then she would be better. It was this baby who was poisoning her.

"If it dies—" she said.

"It's not just the baby. You're also in danger. I better speak to your husband."

"No, I'll talk to him."

She went home, she did what the doctor told her to do. She took the medication. She got into bed. There was a curse on this child, and she, bound to it, surrounding it, surrounded by it, was cursed by it.

She turned over and went to sleep. She slept and slept, only sitting up to take the medication and to eat what Natalie cooked. In her sleep she shut out the world, she shut out knowing, she shut out moving. There had been too much moving, too much knowing already. She sank into a stillness in which everything would be repaired, if she could just stay there long enough.

Natalie woke her up. "The landlady came twice for the rent. I told her you were asleep. She said she'd be back tomorrow."

"I don't have the money to pay her. Maybe we should call the welfare people." But she didn't call them. (She remembered how when she was a child her mother used to pretend that she wasn't getting a relief check, would say that she was getting money from relatives, that they owed her.)

Once more the landlady came, this time with threats. "Tell her I'll have the money for her at the end of the week," Leona said. "Tell her that I've been sick."

When the landlady left, Natalie said, "Momma, you can't keep lying there like that. You're not sick any more. The fever's down. The swelling's down. You've got to get up."

"Not now. Later."

The child within her was moving now, while she wanted nothing so much as to be still. To be still and not to feel all the things she didn't want to feel, about herself, about the baby, that there even was a baby. (Not her baby, Aleida's baby. Huge, spiteful, cunning Aleida, who had directed her once and did still.)

"Please, Momma," Natalie tugged at Leona's arm.

Leona shoved her away. "Stop it!"

Natalie pulled the covers off.

Leona pulled them back again. "Leave me alone! Let me be!"

Natalie grabbed Leona's shoulders, she pulled and she tugged. "Get up! Please, oh, please, get up!"

Looking into Natalie's face, so close, so frightened, Leona saw in her eyes the image of herself, so small.

33

Behind Aleida was the stage with the closed blue curtain. Before her were the women. Above them, the high peaked ceiling.

My space, my studio, she said to herself, feeling how everything was finally going her way.

She was no longer the assistant. She was the one in charge.

For Ninta had simply vanished, as if blown away, in a puff of air. She must never have wanted it—the class, the studio—in the first place if she let it go so easily. It was like taking candy from a baby, (No, no baby . . .) taking Ninta's gestures, her movements, her sequences from her—using them for my own purposes, for the right purposes, Aleida thought gleefully.

Since that night when she had felt so dragged down by Ken into that bottomless hole—had even gone along with being pulled down, as if she was just a puppet, saying, Yes, Yes, do whatever you want with me—she had decided it was going to be up to her to pull herself out. Let him sink, if that was what he wanted. But she wasn't going to let him pull her down with him.

It had come to her that night, suddenly, what it was that she could do. She could teach the women in Peralta, she could teach them movement. But not the old dried up movement, the sterile movement that Ninta had been teaching. No, she could teach them about movement and feeling. Motion and Emotion, the thought came to her, they're even tied in words.

Oh sure, she knew, the women had things, lots of things, houses, new cars, all that stuff that she didn't have. (She still felt spasms of envy about that.) But what she had, that they didn't have, was that she really knew about needing and wanting, knew it to its very core. She was, you might say, the world expert on needing and wanting.

So, all right, these women had their houses and their cars. There still was in them all that they needed and wanted, that they never spoke about or thought about, that maybe they didn't even know about, that they protected themselves from knowing: How they were caged and didn't even know it, how they went along like sheep with their own caging.

Yes, they needed, they needed knowing and moving and feeling, and she was the one who would satisfy that need—in return for payment.

*   *   *

"Lie down on the floor and close your eyes. Try to relax. Forget everything that happened today, what you should have done, what you didn't do. Forget it all and just lie back. Breathe deeply. Let your weight go into the pull of gravity. Feel everything settle into the floor, as if you were sinking. Good. Good.

"We're going to get up slowly, and we're going to keep that sense of relaxation. Let's try a few swings in place, first with the arms. Lift and drop and lift and drop. Easy, easy. Now let the head join in, now the upper body, now from the waist, now the whole body, down and up and down and up. Keep it relaxed, don't rush it. Good. Good. Open yourself up to the feeling of relaxation, of letting go."

After the gentle stretches, she told them to sit down, she told them to lie down, she told them just to breathe easily and to start feeling their feelings, slowly, slowly.

She knew she had to go carefully with them, start out slowly, bring them along bit by bit. She would have to give them time—a few weeks—a month or two. And then, when they were ready, she would take them where she wanted them to go. She didn't like waiting, but she told herself she could stand waiting a while, as long as at the end she knew she would have her own way.

In the meantime, she led them gently, step by step. It was true she didn't know exactly where she was going to take them, but the main thing was that she was going to take them where *she* wanted to. She had on her side all that needing, all that wanting in them, ready to follow the needing and wanting in herself.

She would not be stopped, not this time. She was out in front, way ahead of them all, and nobody was going to take her place.

34

Betrayal—the word kept rushing up in me, not a leaking stain, but a flood, becoming thought's only channel. Each time I felt, heard the word in my mind, an image came along with it: Aleida and Ken standing on a hillside looking down into the meadow, and she, Aleida, pointing down to where I was, pointing at me.

And then the image went further, I pushed it further, to see Aleida and Ken descend into the meadow, both laughing, like twin brother and sister in that laugh, she swaying her hips as she walked, arching her long neck, shaking back her hair, and he, catlike, sinuous and supple, walking toward the White Elephant booth where I—unsuspecting fool—was reaching out for the shawl with metallic threads. . . .

It was like a memory returning, only it wasn't a memory of my own. It was a scene I was directing, while at the same time I was the one who was being directed.

*   *   *

I made breakfast and lunch and dinner, I cleaned and shopped, I did the laundry, I did the gardening, I ferried the kids where they had to go, to the dentist, to swimming lessons, I drove Amy to the Co-op nursery school and took my turn as teacher, I sat with Amy on one side of the table, while Gregg and Rebecca sat on the other, and, at the end of the meal, I asked Gregg what had happened that day at work, I did all the hundred and one things one does in a domestic daily life, you add up the day, you don't know where it's gone, but you have been busy from morning to night; things just go on and on by themselves.

But now, with this—this word, this image—breaking in, each day broke into little bits. There seemed no continuity, no going on. Only this, that, the next thing: I've done this, now I can do that, now I have to do that, starting, stopping, starting, stopping.

Now that Ninta had gone, left without a word to me or to anyone, all that was leftover and unresolved from her class, from what she had said, weighed upon me. I was stuck with something begun but unfinished. It will come, she had said, that sense of going on and on but not only had it not come, now that starting and stopping from the dance class had moved over into my daily life and I was powerless to keep it out. I had been better off before I had begun with her.

I began to wonder if this was the way I had always lived, only I hadn't recognized it. I began to wonder if this was how everybody lived. Did they too have a sense of living in time that was starting and stopping and starting all over again? As if life was always breaking up into little bits.

Or did they have the sense of things going on and on, of life leading them, of things being better, of things always going on to get better and better? So they seemed to feel when I saw them—the women—in the neighborhood, in the park, at the market, at the nursery school.

Once I tried to say something about this to Gregg, how I wondered about other people, how they lived their lives. I said it hesitantly, trying to say and not say at the same time.

Nobody's that different. We're all human beings. We all live the same way, he said. We get up in the morning, we go to work, we come home to our families, same kind of houses, maybe decorated a little differently—

Yes, I persisted, I know that. But that's not what I meant. I wonder what life is like for them—inside themselves.

I don't see how we can possibly know, he said. They don't tell us. They probably can't tell us, anymore than we can tell them.

But you can, I insisted, you can try to put yourself in their place—

You only call it their place, he said with a hint of anger in his voice, but it's still really yours.

35

As Leona approached their—his—house, Felicity came running down the driveway, her belly hanging lower than ever. Felicity rubbed against her leg, turned in a figure eight, came back and rubbed her leg again. Leaning down over her own large stomach to pet her, Leona recalled how the children had laughed. And now she, as well as the cat, was waddling.

Opening the front door with her key—no, he hadn't changed the lock—she peered in uneasily. (Why did she have the almost overpowering sense that she would find that something had happened to him, that he had, yes, killed himself, that she was the one who would find his dead body?) The house was empty, Mike and Zack must still be at school, at baseball practice.

She walked into the living room. How white the couch was, how the black tables and lamps gleamed, how all the surfaces were polished and neat. She didn't remember it being this way, except for the party—No, I am not going to think of the party, she told herself, I have more important things to do. I was a fool, I walked out and let him have everything. I should have told him to go. Why did I feel I was the one who had to go? She went to the window and looked out. How neat the garden was, so well tended. And there were new kinds of flowers blooming, things she didn't recognize at all. Had he taken up gardening? Had he missed her?

She heard the key in the lock. She tried to compose herself, to prepare the speech she was going to make to him. She heard the door opening, she did not turn, she kept looking out at the garden. She wanted him to speak first. She heard instead a cry of terror, a woman's cry. She turned and there was Alice Black, standing in the doorway, carrying a sack of groceries.

"You scared me. I didn't expect anyone."

"I didn't expect to see you," said Leona. She was about to say "in my house," but it was not her house anymore. I was a fool, I walked out and left everything. I should have told him to go.

"I—I've been shopping."

"I can see you've been shopping. So you're doing his shopping now. Secretaries aren't supposed to do shopping, are they?" The harshness in her laugh was like a thawing, or like a cruelty growing in a strange, fertile soil. "What time is he coming home?" she demanded.

"I don't know."

"Is he going ice dancing?" How could she have forgotten about his ice dancing?

"No, he's not going ice dancing. He doesn't go ice dancing any more."

"Oh, he doesn't? Why not?"

"He's too busy, now that—"

"Don't tell me he's become an administrator?"

"A manager," said Alice Black and smiled a smile of pride, an officious smile of pride.

"An administrator," said Leona. Who is she to correct me about him? But then she remembered she had no rights in him any more. She could still say "my husband," but what did that mean? Legally, she told herself, legally we're still married, legally I have some rights.

"Well whatever he is, Mr. Important, I'm not going to wait around here for him to come home."

"You should have called and made an appointment."

"Made an appointment? You must be kidding. He hung up the one time I called him." She felt the baby moving in her body, kicking, moving, turning. "I have something important I have to say to him and I insist on seeing him now." She felt the sound of harshness, of anger, burrowing deeper into her own voice.

"I'll call him and see what he says."

"He'd better come," said Leona.

Alice Black went into the kitchen with the groceries. Leona heard her put the sack on the counter. She heard her dial. She knew what it felt like, she could feel the index finger of her right hand in the holes, she could feel the receiver cradled in her left hand, just as if she were doing it herself. Alice came out again. She said, "He says he's right in the middle of a conference and he doesn't want to be disturbed. He says whatever you want to say to him, you can say by letter."

"Well you just go right back in there and tell him that if he doesn't come here, I'm going to march right over there into the office and say what I have to say in front of everybody. He won't like that much, will he, especially now that he's an administrator?"

Alice Black went back into the kitchen. Leona heard her talking in a low (secretarial) voice. She hung up and came out and said, "He'll be here in a few minutes."

"How nice of him," Leona spat out.

After a long silence, Alice Black said, "Please sit down."

She's asking me to sit down in my own house, thought Leona. "No, thanks, I'll stand."

"Would you like some coffee?"

"If I want a drink, I'll get one myself, thank you very much."

Alice Black went into the kitchen and busied herself with putting the groceries away. Leona heard the refrigerator door open and shut, then open and shut. (And the blood is gone. Oh yes, the blood is gone, of that I'm sure. He must have thrown it down the sink, the whole huge bottle, or would he have thrown it in the garbage? Where should old blood go?)

Suddenly, standing in the living room, or what was once her own living room but was no longer, Leona felt, I am not going to survive this. I must lie down. I must get some rest. She went over to the white couch. She kicked off her shoes. She fell back against the pillows. She closed her eyes. I don't know why I came. I don't know what I'm doing here. I'll go back right away, I won't even talk to him. But she could not get up, she could not make herself move. She tried to remember all the times she had lain on the couch, when she had been so safe here, when life was so easy. Once, that day when it had been so cold out but so warm in the house—after the performance at the Community Theater—when life had seemed just what she wanted it to be, without effort. . . . But the shape of the one who had lain there then (the shape the pillows had taken on) was not the shape of the one who lay here now. Before her, on her, in her, was a huge mound, growing, getting larger, draining the life out of her.

She tried to breathe easily and deeply. She felt herself slipping into sleep, or rather almost into it. She was dreaming that she was in her own house—but she was in her own house—and she was dreaming that someone, something lay upon her chest and she could not breathe, it was stifling her, it, someone was holding her down so she could not move, holding her fast, so she could not get away. She must get up, she must get away, but she could not run away. She was still in the dream, it was holding her fast, and she could not get away.

She heard a noise. The noise was in the dream that she was in. Now she was out of the dream but the noise was still there. The door was being opened, the front door, she knew its sound. She jumped up, she straightened her hair, her clothes over her big belly, so big. She heard Norman's voice asking something, she heard Alice answer quietly.

He came in.

The way he looked was a blow to her. He was no longer boyish. Something had shifted in him in these few months. He had taken a leap from youth to middle age without stopping in between. He slumps like Natalie, she saw. Even as she looked at him, he stared at her in surprise. And she thought, have I too changed that much? Then she remembered the baby. At least I don't have to tell him about that. He can see with his own eyes.

Alice came into the room and stood watching them, as if it were a performance. I have to say the right words, Leona told herself. I don't want to fight with him. I need his help. I have no one else. Doesn't he remember all that we were to each other, all those days, all those nights? How could he remember? She couldn't remember. That man in that different body and she in her different body, they—these two new bodies—had never made love.

"Mike and Zack, how are they?" she asked gently, trying to remind him—and herself—of what they still shared.

"I'm surprised you ask. You didn't worry about them when you went off and deserted them."

Her voice trembled so she could hardly go on. "You wanted me to go, didn't you?"

"Look," he burst out, "I'm taking time off from work. I have to get back right away for an important meeting. Will you get to the point?"

"A meeting?" she said icily. "The administrator goes to a meeting."

"I don't have the time to listen to this, Leona. I'm just going to go if you don't get to the point."

The point, she thought. What is the point? The point is that this is my house and it's not any more. The point is that this is where I used to feel I belonged, I was floating, held up, and now I feel as if it's here that I'm drowning. "I need money for the baby," she said.

"Why are you asking me for money for your baby?"

His savagery astonished her. "My baby? (It's not my baby.) It's your baby. I'm six months along. You can count back. You know how to count, don't you? That night before I left we—we were together." She could not say, we made love. Where was love in this room, with that secretary watching?

If I could, I would tear this child out of me and give it to him.

Her heart was pounding in rage, in terror, in she didn't know what, she could hardly breathe. She felt herself wobbling on an edge, about to drop into a narrow space, clotted with darkness, meant for falling and more falling. Desperately she said to him, "There can be proof, you know, there's such a thing as a blood test?"

"Norman," Alice said.

"Please stay out of this, Alice."

"Yes, you stay out of this. It's none of your business what he and I say to each other. Why are you hanging around here anyhow?"

"Norman, tell her," Alice said.

"Tell me what?" Leona said to Norman.

An odd smile came over Norman's face. Then as if he were trying to brush it away, he shrugged his shoulders.

"It just happens to be my business, since Norman and I are now living together."

Leona looked at Norman and then at Alice. She

couldn't believe it. This mousy woman, this colorless woman, this officious woman was living with Norman? She began to laugh. She laughed and laughed, she could not stop laughing. If I am not careful, I am going to wet my pants, she told herself. She sat down on the couch. It was never Aleida, why did I think it was Aleida, it was always this woman, this sexless woman, it was she who broke up my marriage. But what kind of marriage was it then, if it could be so easily broken by her? Now she was laughing and sobbing, sobbing and laughing, wiping the tears from her face with the back of her hand.

She looked up, she saw on their faces uneasiness, disgust, and fear. She is afraid of me, she thought, and he is afraid of me too. Was he always afraid of me?

"All right, I'll send you some money every month but I want you to stay away from me," Norman said, his lips thin and tight.

Now, finally, he was disconnected from her and she was disconnected from him. She would never again be able to think of him with that closeness that brought his skin against her skin, his voice to her ears, his hands to her hands. A death, it was like a death.

Her mouth and throat were so dry she could not swallow. Yet she had to swallow. "I need some water."

"I'll get it," said Alice.

"No, I'll get it."

She went into the kitchen, she went to the cabinet and slid open the door. She saw the dishes lined up in careful rows. My dishes, she eats off my dishes. In her hands she felt the memory of hundreds of days of putting food on them, of setting them on the table, of scraping the leftovers off, of rinsing them, of putting them in the dishwasher, of taking them out when they were dry, of putting them away. She had always put the ones with the chips on the bottom, yet somehow they always seemed to make their way to the top.

She took out a glass. She turned on the faucet. She let the water run. She filled the glass. She drank the whole glass at one gulp. Then she filled the glass again and drank another glass. She put the glass down on the counter.

Let her wash it.

She went back into the living room. They were standing there, the two of them, close to each other, as if they'd just been whispering. Allies, she thought, against me. She looked out on the garden. She thought of the blood that she had poured upon the cyclamen and the fuchsias and the camellias and the rhododendron and of the wonderful colors of their blooms.

My child, not Aleida's child, she thought.

36

After the series of movements, the relaxations, the stretches, the runs and leaps, came the time, once more, for talk. "Today let's see what happens if we work on the word 'aggression,' on what it is to move and feel aggressively. I know and you know that it's not considered nice to be aggressive in the real world. But here, in this class, nobody's going to sit in judgment on your for not being 'nice.' Here you can allow yourself to express everything that comes with not being 'nice.' Only then—when you can feel your own feelings, not the feelings that somebody else has forced on you and said, 'Here, feel these'—will you finally be able to move the way you were meant to move. That's what it's all about, motion and emotion," Aleida ended, stirred by her own passionate words.

"Any questions? No? Then, let's start. Everybody stand up. Now, somebody give me an example of an aggressive action—a word, I mean."

"Hitting."

"Okay."

"Shoving."

"Striking."

"Stamping."

"Kicking."

"Scratching."

"Good. Good. Now I'd like each one of you to take one of those words, any word that suits you, and start moving with the feeling of that word. See how it makes you move, and see how it makes you feel when you move that way. See what new feelings are brought up, and how those new feelings push you on to even more moving—maybe even a different kind of movement."

First one woman, then another, began to move, striking out, then pulling back, then striking out at the empty air. Just looking at them she could see how fearful they were. As if the moment they put out their hand it might get cut off or as if the water in front of them was too deep and they were afraid to get their feet wet—

"Remember what I told you. You don't have to be nice here. Nobody's going to condemn you, no matter what you do. What are you risking? It's just a dance class, right?"

Some of the women began to push and jab at the air. It was beginning to come now, but it was still constipated, constricted. Tiny movements, fearful movements, needy movements, imitations of imitations. How mousy they looked, how they were prisoners of what they'd been told to believe. She felt a moment of caution, but she shook it off impatiently. I'm just going to push them harder. It's time.

"Look," she said. "Why don't you imagine for yourself that someone is being aggressive to you? I'm sure it's happened to you, it's happened to everybody, that they get pushed around unfairly. Remember how sick you felt about it. Remember how you were the victim. Identify with that. You've been screwed, but now it's time for you to fight back."

"No, no, no, no," she stopped them a moment later. "It's still too nice. What are you doing with these tiny slaps? They'd never get you out of anywhere. Look—No, wait a minute, let's try something else. Suppose it's not just for yourself that you're doing this. Suppose there's something that's threatening to destroy everything you have—your house, your children, your husband, every-thing. And supposed that their survival depends on your fighting this thing off. Then could you do that? Could you fight back? Could you be not nice?"

Now they changed. Their motions became harder, sharpers. They were pushing and shoving, kicking and scratching, hitting heavily at the air. The movements were taking on a life and a force of their own.

"Good, good," Aleida called out. "It's getting better, much better. But you don't have to stay put in one place. You can start moving throughout the space. This is your space to move in, this entire space, this hall. Make it yours."

Now they are really getting it, now they are beginning to look as if they mean it, Aleida thought, caught up in the watching, caught up in the feeling that she (I, she thought, I) had done this. Here, in her studio, in her class, look at them now, thrashing out, kicking, throwing themselves at the air, pounding at it, lashing it, cutting it. Watching them, she felt that she was moving them, that their moving was her moving.

If Ninta came in now, to what used to be her studio— but was no more—what would she say, seeing all the pounding, and lashing, all the kicking out? She would probably pee in her pants. She would probably jump out of her skin, afraid that she was being contaminated.

Her and her stupid ideas about motion. Pure motion. There was no such thing. Bodies were bodies.

The thought came to her of her mother, as she was at the end—so frail, so light, her skin almost transparent, as she lay in the hospital bed. And when the male nurse tried to move her to a chair, she'd cried out, I'm going to fall, Am I going to fall?

No, she would not remember that.

She did not have to remember that.

She was here in her own studio, telling them, showing them how to move. She was no longer the one who had been replaced at the head of the line. She was the one now who had done the replacing.

37

Across the intersection, in the driver's seat of an old red car, I saw Aleida and I felt a spasm of rage. The light turned green, the red car passed me in the opposite lane. I saw the driver was not Aleida. But the cramp of rage did not ease; it tightened. It stayed with me, coiled about the image of sharply sloping shoulders, of that arrogant lean of the head, of eyes so dark they seemed to start out of their whites.

*   *   *

I was standing by the kitchen window, looking out on the garden. I saw a gray cat in the shadow of the dark purple dodonea. I saw a mockingbird swoop down to touch the cat's tail, arc up swiftly, then swoop down again, this time skimming so low it ruffled the fur on the cat's back. I saw the cat shake her head; she looked off into space as if she had not noticed what the bird had done.

I knew that the cat that stood so dumbly, unmoving, not at all like a cat, knew about the nest of baby birds in the dodonea. For all its pretending to be so meek, at the moment a baby bird would try to fly, the cat would leap, would become the powerful predator.

I had seen feathers in the grass often enough.

It was not a matter of fault. How could a cat choose not to obey instinct? Yet I would still feel pity (Was that too instinct?), seeing the scattered feathers, the broken neck, the staring, dead eyes of the baby bird.

Who can help feeling pity for a victim, for any victim? Who can refuse to help a victim, when you see her or him before you?

I recalled that night in the bathroom of the Community Theater. I had seen Leona weep, I had decided to talk to Aleida for her. Was it pity that made me do what I did, become intermediary for her to the one tormenting her, because I felt what she felt, had put myself in her place?

Or was Gregg right, was it only pity for myself that I had been feeling? Was I never able—would I never be able to move outside myself, condemned instead to an isolation that allowed a pretense of pity, that called itself identification, called itself love?

I turned away from the window.

Ketz.

* * *

At night I dreamed I was with a group of tourists, who had taken over a castle at the top of a mountain illegally. I did not want to be accused with them of a crime that they, not I, had committed. I hurried outside to make my escape before the true owners came. I ran along a dirt path that sloped down the side of the mountain. At the bottom, barely visible, in the distance was a beautiful small village. Halfway down, I suddenly turned back. I realized that I knew no one in that village. What made me think they would welcome me? At least the tourists in the castle were not total strangers to me. Reentering the castle, I saw a man standing alone, deep in thought. He did not notice me, though I passed directly in front of him.

I went into the kitchen of the castle. It was surprisingly small and dark. Against one wall was a free-standing cupboard. It was jutting out at a perilous angle away from the wall. At any moment it could fall crashing to the floor, shattering the dishes and glasses within it.

Backing away, I felt my foot brush against something. I looked down and saw a side of beef on the floor, the fat glistening. Beside it was a bill, made out in my name.

Are you the one who made out this bill to me? I asked a woman who was crouched in the corner.

Yes, the woman said.

I did not order this, I want it out, I raged.

* * *

It was after the children had gone to bed. Gregg was pacing up and down the cork-tiled floor of the living room (still that smell of mold, still faint, no worse). Looking at him, though he was not looking at me, I saw an expression come and go on his face, an unfamiliar expression, one I could not locate in our past history. It was not quite a smile. It was more the prevention of a smile.

I shivered, thinking, I am the one who has the secret, not he.

Betrayal, the word came, in my ears, on my tongue, unspoken.

Stop it, I said to myself (as if words could be stopped

by other words). Betrayal is too large a word, suited only to wars and suffering and death.

* * *

We were sitting at the dinner table. Gregg was talking about some new developments in the components of the machine, how now, with new solid-state devices, things were going to go faster, how everything would be simpler, smaller. His smile that wasn't a smile came, went, was back again. There was in him now, I could see, a new quality, something close to gloating—I could see it so clearly in him, I didn't need him to say it—that things were going to be different now, not only in Peralta but in the world because of what he—and the others with him—were doing at work.

Yes, I told Rebecca and Amy, yes, they could leave the table.

I felt a revulsion against all outside triumphs—outside myself, outside this house. Why was it that what was outside always won out over everything else? (Pity, pity for the victims.)

I turned back to him. (He was outside, outside with his triumph in the world.) I saw him with other eyes, caustic eyes, baleful, cutting, negating, eyes, seeing all that he said with revulsion.

What did I know—what had I ever known—of triumph in the world? Except that cut off from it, I hated it . . . hated him?

No, I must not let myself feel this way. I was being unfair to him. What was wrong with his wanting to do well, to succeed? Why should I begrudge him this triumph when it was his work, his success, that made this life possible for the children, for me?

It was his work upon which I depended for my very existence. I should be grateful.

But I was not grateful.

Bitterness, accusation, went on and on; it would not stop, kept going further and further. It came to me that all the time that I felt guilty, tormented myself about my betrayal of him, another kind of betrayal had been going on. I had been betraying myself, believing that my moving mattered, when I had never moved in the real world, only stopped, started, and stopped again. All the time in the outside world, real movement was making its real mark, erecting real monuments, pushing, shoving, discarding whatever it was ready to discard of the unmoving, the powerless, shattering, using, misusing . . .

Ketz. Ketz. Ketz. Unfair, unfair, unfair.

But rage, cramping within me, would not listen. It had taken up permanent residence in me. It was the lasting fuel of motion.

When I got up in the morning, I tried to leave it there on the sheet behind me, I wanted to leave it, but it came with me, was with me when I least wanted to think of it.

It was like a story that had gotten started and would not stop, a story that had dispensed with everything but itself, even the narrator.

38

It was our nightly ritual. First there was a story (This night, it was the end of *Charlotte's Web*), then there was a song, an old one ("Hush little baby, don't you cry . . .") I saw—I felt Amy's breathing become soft as she drifted into sleep. But as I tucked Rebecca in I noticed that her eyes looked glazed, dull. I touched her forehead. It was cool.

Does Rebecca look all right to you? I asked Gregg, as I came out into the hallway. She looks fine to me, he said, same as usual.

In the middle of the night there was a cry. I jumped out of sleep, out of bed, and ran into the children's room to find Rebecca in the midst of a fever dream, standing beside the bed, unable to say what was, what was not, pointing at the edge of the bed, weeping. I tried to soothe her. She shrank away from me. She did not want me to come close to her.

I persuaded her to let me give her a cool bath to bring the fever down, I gave her an aspirin.

In the morning the fever was still high.

I took her to the doctor. He examined her, he thought it was not a bacterial infection, but he would take a culture anyhow. He said, Give her aspirin; he said, Give her fluids; he said, Call me in the morning.

*   *   *

The illness of a child, the sudden abyss—the falling into illness as the only daily life. You spend your time moving, you cannot stop, going in and out of the sick child's room, trying to comfort though she will not be comforted, trying to amuse, though she will not be amused. How she is so distant, the child in illness. How she falls into sleep, wakes, calls out, I want it fixed, and begins to cry. There are wrinkles in the sheet, she says, sitting up, Smooth them out, smooth them out. Yet when you smooth them out, it is not right, she still wants it fixed.

Day and night you go in and out of the room. You touch her forehead as she sleeps. It seems cooler, but is it cooler? You have fallen into the tyranny of omen. If I had done this . . . If I had not done that. . . .

*   *   *

On the fifth day the fever broke. (Yes, it had been a virus, not a bacterial infection.)

Rebecca became irritable, wanted to get up, began fighting with Amy, said, No, you can't use that purple crayon, it's mine.

Things were as they had been, almost as they had been.

*   *   *

I reassembled my daily life. I did what I had to do. I maintained what had to be maintained. Duty must now, more than ever, not be refused. (What had I been doing? What had I been thinking?)

This—in here—this house, this space, all that I had helped to build day by day by the simplest and most repetitive of actions, a placing of a mat on a table, of a spoon and a fork and a knife and a napkin upon the mat, a pouring out of milk from a bottle after first shaking it, to mix the cream with the bluer lower liquid—this is what I should be thinking of.

In the future, soon, at any moment, I might be called to account, asked, What did you do with what you have been given? Dishes, glasses, pots, pans, silverware, the floors, the very walls in the house, the bathroom sink, the tub, the mirrors, the books, the dresses, pants, everything that was in closets, even things stored away, the outside of the house, its walls, the garden . . . your life . . . What have you done with it?

(Have you kept the children intact, undamaged? Have you allowed them to become what they need to be, unhindered? What have you done with them, for them, they who are part of yourself, were once in your body, but now are not you, are separate from you?)

* * *

I dreamed I was in a house with many others, all of them unknown to me; I was once again a child. Someone in the house, a woman, a man, was giving a lesson in movement in the kitchen. He, she, spoke of discovering the meaning of movement.

I said, I used to move well but no longer.

The man-woman said to me, You should leave, I wouldn't stay if I were you.

*   *   *

I was working in the back corner of the garden where I had first planted wild strawberry—It had flowered white, then died—and after that hypericum—It had flowered yellow, then died. Even the vinca, which I had put in last month when the nursery man told me it was very hardy, was barely surviving. Only a few purple flowers appeared here and there on skimpy plants, surrounded by ugly weeds.

I began to pull at the taller weeds. They broke off at ground level. With a long sharp tool, I forced my way through the thick crust of dried adobe to root them out. As the wheelbarrow filled with scraggly stalks, so quickly gone limp, I dug more and more intently. How hard it was to work in this clay. It was always either too dry or too muddy. It was never the way dirt should be, soft and friable.

The tool hit against something hard. I kept digging, my arm and wrist and fingers sore from the effort. Finally I unearthed what was hidden there. It was only an old brick, a half of a brick.

Once, before the tract was built, there had been a farm here. (And before that?) Then the developer had come in and cleared the land and leveled it, covering over a life once lived, so all that remained to tell of that life were buried stones, half-bricks.

39

It was ten-thirty at night. I was sitting on the couch in the family room, sewing the hem of a purple skirt made of Mexican cotton. Lying back in his Barwa lounge chair, Gregg was reading. He laughed, loudly.

"What's so funny?" I asked, automatically.

He tilted the lounge chair forward so he was sitting up. "I told you about this book, *Flatland*, didn't I?"

"No," I said.

"I thought I did. It's been out of print for years. I first read it when I was in high school. I remember loving it then. But I could never find a copy. Now they've reissued it. It's about a society which exists in only two dimensions. All the inhabitants are also two-dimensional, different kinds of geometric shapes. The men are divided into various classes or functions for which there are different shapes, triangles or squares or pentagons. But the women are all one class. They're all the same, they're straight lines."

"Straight lines? That doesn't seem—"

"Listen, listen to this part: 'If our highly pointed Triangles of the Soldier class are formidable, it may be readily inferred that far more formidable are our

Women. For if a Soldier is a wedge, a Woman is a needle; being, so to speak, *all* point, at least at the two extremities ...' "

"But—"

"Wait a minute. Just let me finish. 'Add to this the power of making herself practically invisible at will, and you will perceive that a Female, in Flatland, is a creature by no means to be trifled with. Not that it must be for a moment supposed that our Women are destitute of affection. But unfortunately the passion of the moment predominates, in the Frail Sex, over every other consideration. This is, of course, a necessity arising from their unfortunate conformation. For as they have no pretensions to an angle, being inferior in this respect to the very lowest of the Isoceles, they are consequently devoid of brainpower and have neither reflection, judgment nor forethought, and hardly any memory.

" 'Hence, in their fits of fury, they remember no claims and recognize no distinctions. I have actually known a case where a Woman has exterminated her whole household, and half an hour afterwards, when her rage was over and the fragments swept away, has asked what has become of her husband and her children.' " He looked up and laughed again.

"You think that's funny?"

"Oh come on. It is funny. It's a very clever following out of a mathematical proposition to its ultimate consequences. It's a mathematical *tour de force.*" He leaned back in the chair.

"It may be a *tour de force* but I still don't think it's funny." I notice a small drop of blood forming on the index finger of one hand. I must have pricked myself with the needle.

Gregg sat forward in the chair, he shut the book, he

got out of the chair. He stood looking at me, his arms folded. The light glinted on his glasses. I looked away.

"What's the matter with you these days? You are in a really foul mood. You take everything I say, even something I read to you, as an attack. I was only reading it to you because I thought it would make you laugh. I think it's funny. You would think so, too, if you took the trouble to think about it, instead of jumping on it—first thing—because I said it."

I did not answer him. I put my finger to my mouth and sucked the blood.

"You carry everything too far," he said and went out of the room.

I put my sewing down. I got up. I went over to the floor-to-ceiling window and looked out into the darkness. I saw the reflections of the lights in the room superimposed upon the dark mounds of the bushes.

I thought, Yes, I have gone too far.

I went into the bedroom. He was lying there, the light on, his eyes closed, one arm thrown over his forehead, the covers twisted over him. I took it into myself, this gesture, as if it were a wound of my own, calling for pity, calling for apology.

I went over to him. I stood beside the bed. I said, "I'm sorry, I don't know—"

He opened his eyes. Without his glasses he was very nearsighted; his eyes seemed soft and dreamy. He put his hand out to me. He said, "Are you just about to get your period?"

I said, "I don't think so. But my period has been very irregular lately. Maybe that's it."

I lay beside him. He put his arms around me. I assured myself, Rage has no place here.

Yet even as I thought this—(thought?), felt this—(feeling?), I was overtaken, entirely unexpectedly by a rush of intense desire. I was remembering that night in the motel with Ken. Why had this memory come now, why especially now, when I had not even thought of him, felt desire for him. Had I ever felt desire for him?

Afterwards I knew memory had had its own way with me, detached from thought, from ordinary feeling, a property of body alone. I did not feel guilt so much as despair at the intransigence of body, that all the time had been readying itself with this secret. In the midst of the act of love, a secret that locked out access to anything but itself, encased in a covering of the most porous skin, and yet at the same time penetrating, all point, all point.

I got up. I went into the family room. I went over to the floor-to-ceiling window and looked out into the dark mounds piled upon darker mounds.

I felt a sense of rancor, a sense of threat, a sense of being betrayed, a sense of being the betrayer, a sense of too prolonged waiting, a sense of bitter hilarity, of sullenness, of cramping. I felt my foot wanting to kick out to smash the glass.

40

Sitting in the frayed green upholstered chair in the small dark flat, Leona felt the sudden tightening, the sudden pulling down and in of a contraction. She held her breath. It let go and she let go; she sighed in relief. Is it finally time? she wondered. No, the contractions had been going on for days, small ones, stopping. How long this pregnancy had gone on, nothing like any of the others, how she wanted it to be over, to have her own body back to itself, for herself.

Laboriously she pulled herself out of the chair. It was time for her appointment to see the doctor. Should she take her things, just in case? No, she didn't want to take her things yet, she could always come back and get them.

Outside the door, she stood on the landing. She looked down the stairs. They were so steep. About to descend, she assured herself, I'm not going to fall. But as she put her foot down on the first step, she wobbled. Only by catching hold of the railing, did she save herself from tumbling. Her heart began to pound. She descended step by step, gingerly, looking down, clutching the railing. Once, if she could have, she would have killed this child, but it was not possible any longer, it was ready to be

born. If she hurt the child now, she would hurt herself.
If she hurt herself, she would hurt the child.

* * *

"It's almost time." The doctor said, turning away. He
had finished his examination.

"How can it be time? It's too early, three weeks too
early. I'm not ready."

"You don't have much choice, Mrs. Thayer. I suggest
you go home and get your things and get on over to the
hospital."

As she dressed, she thought of all the things she hadn't
gotten: I don't have a single receiving blanket or shirt or
even a diaper. He's wrong. I'm sure he's wrong. The contractions yesterday and today were mild, hardly more
than a small tightening. If it's anything, it's false labor.
He's wrong. I have plenty of time. All my labors are long.

She put her hand on her swollen belly. Wait, wait, she
said, I'm not ready.

* * *

It was crowded in Macy's. Bells were ringing, people
were shoving. Leona made her way in and out among
the other shoppers to the escalator. At the third floor
she got off and walked toward Infant's Wear, but first
she had to go through Toddler's. She passed a rack with
a group of green corduroy dresses, each with a lace col-
lar. How beautiful the color was and the lace. She lingered. Later, she said to herself, as if it were a promise
to the baby. She knew it was going to be a girl, there was
no doubt in her mind, she felt it to be so, it had something to do with the way she was carrying it, so high.

She made herself go on to Infant's Wear. She saw shirts and receiving blankets. How many should she get?

Now.

It came. It was coming. Yes, now she remembered exactly how it was the other times, that feeling of being pressed down upon, a world of nothing but inside pressing to get outside.

It stopped.

She let out her breath. It was nothing, nothing. It didn't take hold, it didn't go any further.

In a display case just behind the counter she saw a beautiful white garment, a precious covering, made to completely encase the baby, except for its face. "How much is that? Can I see that?" she asked the salesgirl, pointing.

"It's thirty-nine dollars."

It was far too expensive, but it was so beautiful. No, I can't get it, Leona decided. I have to be practical. She took the escalator down to the first floor and found a phone booth and put a nickel in the slot. The phone kept ringing and ringing. No answer. Why isn't Natalie back from school? Did I dial a wrong number? She dialed again, saying the numbers to herself as she put her right index finger in each hole of the rotating dial. Seven, five, two, one, eight, three, four.

No answer. She hung up. She'd try again in five minutes.

It was White Flower Day and everywhere there were bargains. In Women's Shoes she picked up a beautiful black patent pump with white linen trim. She turned it over and looked at the price. Twenty-nine-ninety-five. It was no bargain, it was still too expensive. A smartly dressed woman in a long full skirt with a tight waist picked up the shoe after Leona put it down and asked the salesclerk to see it in six-and-a-half A. Leona felt as if she didn't belong in the world.

She went back to the phone booth and called the number—her number again. The only answer to the ring was still silence.

Now.

It came again, pressing harder, pulling down deeper, holding longer, as if it was not going to let go. But it did let go.

What should she do now? Go home? Go to the hospital? She couldn't decide. She couldn't stay in the phone booth. Someone was outside, waiting to use it. Let them wait. She tried again. She heard the receiver picked up, she heard Natalie's hesitant, frightened phone voice. "Where were you?" Leona shouted. "Why weren't you home? I told you to be home, in case I needed you."

"The teacher—"

"Never mind the teacher. I need you to come right now with my things. I made up that little case with my stuff, you know where it is. In the closet. I'm at Macy's. Meet me at the Information Booth and hurry."

"But why don't I meet you at the hospital, it would—"

"Do what I tell you for once, will you? Meet me at the Information Booth and hurry!"

Why does she have to aggravate me so much, even now? Leona pushed back the folding door of the booth and brushed past a gray-haired woman who was waiting.

Passing a mirror on the cosmetics counter, Leona saw her own face, so strained looking, her hair so limp, she hardly knew herself. It's the light, the hateful light in department stores, it makes you look so old, it shows every wrinkle, every blemish.

She went back to the escalator. She held tight to the moving railing, grateful to be carried up. That beautiful covering, it would welcome the baby into the world, show her that she belongs, make up for all the mistakes I made in the beginning. But almost a week's budget? Looking down from the escalator onto the second floor, she saw the glasses and the plates set out on tables in House-wares. I have only glasses that are chipped and that don't match. And my plates—Alice Black is using my plates.

At the third floor, stepping off, she misjudged. The unmoving floor appeared too quickly. She tripped and went down on one knee. A woman tried to help her up. "I'm all right, thank you, I can manage," she said. I can manage, I can manage, she repeated to herself as she walked toward Infant's Wear, but she feared for the baby.

Once again she looked at shirts and receiving blankets. She selected two of each and went to the salesgirl at the counter. She tried not to look at the white garment behind the counter.

Now.

Hard, harder, was this the hardest, her body was being squeezed in, out, up, down, she couldn't tell the direction any more. She wanted to lie down, she wanted to push it all away, she wanted to press herself against anything immovable.

It stopped, it was over, she was drenched with relief.

"I'll take that thing too," she gasped, pointing to the white garment.

With the maroon shopping bag in hand, she took the escalator down to the first floor and rushed over to the Information Booth. What was keeping Natalie? Had she gotten lost? Leona looked at the listings in front of her of all the things in the store, all the *L*'s, Lingerie, Luggage—

"Mom, I'm here. Didn't you see me?"

"Where's my case?" Leona cried out.

"I forgot the case but I didn't want to go back, it was too late."

"Oh, for God's sake. Come on, hurry, come on."

Outside at the curb she found a cab. She got into the back seat with Natalie and gave the driver the name and address of the hospital. I have time, I have plenty of time, she told herself. But why was the cab so slow, why was the traffic so bad? The meter was ticking away. She looked at the back of the driver. She saw how stiffly he held his neck.

"Can't you go faster?"

"What do you want me to do, lady, leap over the other cars?"

"I could go faster by walking," she said.

They were standing still, caught in traffic, and she saw the meter ticking away. Two dollars. Two dollars and five cents. Two dollars and ten cents. Two dollars and fifteen cents for nothing but delay. "Pull up here," she said to the driver.

"I can't pull up. There's no place at the curb."

"Then just leave me off here."

She took three dollars out of her purse and handed it to him. He took it and she waited. "Where's my change?" she said harshly.

He raised his right arm without turning. For a moment she thought he was going to reach back and hit her. But instead he flicked his wrists and the coins showered onto the floor of the back seat. Peering down into the darkness, Leona saw them glint like shining centers on the dark mat, and she thought of all that had been scattered that she had stooped to pick.

Natalie leaned over and reached with her hand for a coin. "Don't touch them," Leona yelled. "Leave them where they are."

She pulled herself out of the cab and started walking on the sidewalk, hurrying, pushing by people, bumping them with the maroon shopping bag. It was only a few blocks more. Behind her was Natalie, running to keep up with her.

Now.

It came again. Harder. Harder. It was not going to let

go this time. She was in a vise, she was being forced down through a hole, the baby, herself, the baby, herself. We cannot get through. She felt a wetness descending, a wetness coming out of her, dripping down her legs. She stood there and looked down at the small pool of liquid that had formed on the sidewalk.

41

I dreamed that a dark woman has appeared to lead me away, out of this room, out of this house, down one street, along another, further and further away till we come to a city, a building, an elevator, the door of an apartment high up, another room. Here in this room, where I have come with no protest, I am to be held hostage. Why wasn't I suspicious? I ask myself. Why didn't I tell someone, why didn't I call out on the street?

I see a baby in the corner of the room. The dark woman must not see this baby. I must distract her, must move to keep her attention to me. But I cannot move, I am rooted in place. I cannot even cry out. The woman is turning. No, no, she must not see—but she does see the baby. She runs over to him, she picks him up, she carries him, dangling by one arm, to the open window. In one fierce motion she has cast him out.

I run to the window. I look down many stories. I expect to see, I tremble to see blood and crushed bones below. But the baby has not fallen to the ground. He has been caught in the branches of a high tree. Even now, as I watch, the baby begins to change. He is no longer a baby but a child, strong enough to hang onto the branches, strong enough to climb down the tree, getting older as he climbs. I turn and see the dark woman is standing beside me. She is peering out of the window, absorbed in the transformation of the child. I grab her arms, I pin them behind her. The woman struggles but I hold on with all my strength. Get help, get help, I cry out, I can't hold her much longer, help me.

42

Never had it rained so hard and so long in Peralta—day after day, week after week, till the ground, saturated by the runoff from the hills, shunted off the water in muddy rivulets. In the lowest places in town the water seeped into the houses. Here a piano stood, its legs in the silty dregs, there the level rose to the box spring of a bed. And the clouds hung so low over the valley the foothills could not be seen.

Standing at the living room window, looking out onto

the flooded front garden, Aleida felt an intense excitement, as if the rising water was floating her up out of
the debris of her own life. She was about to be set free
and they, her students, would be set free with her. She
and they, they and she, all together, all mixed up together.

She lay on the couch, the couch with the hole in it,
covered by the blanket that moved and wrinkled when-
ever she moved. I hate this place, she thought, looking
at the plaster ceiling where the stain from the leak was
now spreading. Soon the ceiling will come down. Let it
come down, she hoped. I am going to get out of here
soon, I am going to break away for good.

She thought of all the places she could go, all the possibilities. She put herself in this place, in that place, in
the other, in New York, in Los Angeles, in San Francisco,
in Hawaii, in Europe. The possibilities frightened her,
even as they excited her. She wondered, But will I be
safe in those places, safe as I am here? For here in this
room, this house, though she hated it, it was safe.

I'll just have to wait, she told herself, wait a little longer. I can't plan yet. I'm not ready yet. But still she found
herself trying to plan. She went over and over the same
ground in her mind.

Hearing the rain drumming on the roof, going on and
on, not stopping, she began to grow drowsy. She fell into
a dream of her mother, younger, much younger than she
had been at the time of her death. Now she was well, not
frail, full of vigor. Now she had a baby, and she, Aleida,
was supposed to take care of it while her mother went
to work.

I can't do it, I won't do it, I have to leave here soon,
she protested.

He's got to be taken care of, her mother said.

It's your child, not my child.

You'll do what I say, her mother said to her, pinching her on the arm so hard that a great red welt formed.

Her mother opened the door. She said, I'll be back at the usual time.

What is the usual time? Aleida raged, but her mother was gone.

She looked at the baby, a little boy; he looked at her, knowing, smirking, powerful even thought he was so little.

If she thinks I'm going to hang around and take care of her baby, she has another think coming. I'm going to go. I'm going to leave him alone—

She started out of sleep, but the dream still clung to her. She looked up at the ceiling, she saw the spreading stain. She heard a sound. Ken was standing in the doorway, looking at her. She sat up, as if she had been caught doing something she shouldn't have, but it was he who had come back too soon.

"Why are you home?"

"That son of a bitch Cornog told me he didn't like the way I'd organized the report. He insisted I do it all over again."

"So what did you do?"

He laughed. "I didn't do anything. I said if he didn't like it the way it was, he could redo it himself." He laughed again.

"He's going to pay you, isn't he? Isn't he?" she repeated, as he went out of the room without answering. He went into the kitchen. She heard him open the refrigerator, then slam it shut. He stood in the doorway.

"Is he going to pay you?"

"I don't give a damn if he does or doesn't."

He went over to the window. With his back to her he said, "I think it's time to move."

"To move? Where?"

He turned and gestured outward with his hand. "Some

place. Any place. Away from here. This place is not for me."

"But I'm not ready to leave. I'm just getting my classes going. I've waited a long time for this. I don't want to give it up now."

He was silent. He got out a cigarette, lit it and blew smoke in the air. There was the smell of the smoke and the smell of him in the smoke, of his body in the smoke, of the smoke in his body. He looked at her and smiled his seductive, his sickeningly seductive smile. No, she thought, he's not going to get me so easily as that.

"I don't see why we have to keep on moving," she said, keeping her voice cold.

He sat in the Morris chair. He leaned back against the cracked leather. "I'm not interested in settling down. I don't want to settle down. I want to keep moving. That's one thing I learned in the War, you don't let yourself—"

"Don't start that again. Not the War again. Why do you keep harping on that? That's all over and done with, what happened to you, what happened to your friends. Something weird's going on with you. You ought to go and see a psychiatrist."

"I don't need a psychiatrist."

"Then why do you keep talking about it? It's as if," she shivered, "as if you loved the killing."

"I didn't love the killing. I had no choice."

"I don't think I could ever kill."

"You'd be surprised what you can do, if you have to ... if there are only two choices, to survive or not to survive ..."

"Is it so terrible to want to do more than survive?" she started to say but she saw he wasn't listening. He was doing that thing with his hand again, with his fingers, looking at the ceiling.

Shaking, she went to the window and looked out on

the sodden, wretched garden. All her excitement, all her hopes seemed to have vanished.

She heard him get up. He came up behind her. She held herself still. She did not turn. She felt him running his hand through her hair, touching the back of her neck, rubbing it, leading her on with the promise of the sweet dark pleasure of acquiescing to him, of being pulled down with him.

How was this happening to her, just now when she was so close to getting away? She had thought it was never going to happen to her again, this longing to leap into darkness with him, to fall into his losing with him.

A leftover from another world, that was what he was.

It's nothing but habit, she warned herself, as she saw the signs of her own succumbing. You fell into it so many times before, so now you're falling again. You don't have to let it happen.

But she could not, would not, stop it from happening.

She wanted it. She wanted him.

Though in the last second, just before she gave in to it, just before she let go, she promised herself, This is the last time, the very last time.

43

They drove up the narrow winding road into the hills, past the first gate to the city's property, up to the top of the ridge, and then down the other side, on another twisting narrow road to the lower gate, marked by a sign, "No Trespassing."

They parked outside the gate and climbed over it. Aleida in the lead, followed by her four favorite students, walked down a muddy path through a stand of trees that opened out to a small meadow that led to another gate, another path, another meadow. They walked further until they reached a second stand of trees, where the ground was sodden from the rains. Now the path rose steeply. On the right, the edge dropped away to a deep ravine. From far below, they could hear the sound of running water, a brook swollen by the rains, rushing over large and small boulders.

They climbed steadily, Aleida setting the pace, to where the path widened out to a small plateau, encircled by stumps of decaying trees. In the deeply filtered light they were like shadows of the green stillness.

Aleida took off her shoes. She felt the damp roughness of the ground under her bare feet. It was like new energy streaming up within her. She had had enough of floors, of rooms, of being shut in.

She was filled with a wave of revulsion at what she had been—a victim, a fool, the scapegoat of her own timidity, never willing or able to refuse, him or anyone else.

But no more. That was the last time. Something—cravenness?—had been used up in her.

Now, finally, she was ready to cut herself loose, to break out. What was she going to do? She didn't know yet, but it didn't matter. She was going to start all over again, here, now. This she knew, this she was sure of, she was not going to do what she had done before.

She began to move.

The smallest movements, a tilt of the head, the opening of a hand, the raising of a shoulder, the curling of a fist. Small, so small, yet the gestures began to travel from her to them, her four favorite students. She the leader, they the followers, like disciples, yes, disciples, she thought, half in awe at herself, at her power over them.

Now she began to sway from side to side. And they, holding fast to her every gesture, mirroring her, swayed rhythmically, from side to side. It was like a wave flowing through them, a motion with a life all its own, her own, going on and on outward, bringing other movements into play, movements you could never have imagined in your mind.

If Ken were here now, what would he say? How he made fun of what she was trying to do, called it "The Ladies Emoting." But if he saw them now, he would see he had been wrong, all wrong, that she was the one who had been right.

"Move more. Move more," she called out. Mirroring her, they jumped and turned, arms and legs and torso and head moving percussively, sharply. It ran through them all, like jerky fire, this angularity.

No, even if he were standing right there, watching

them, he still wouldn't believe it, that was the way he was, he would try to pass it off as a joke. In the middle of their moving he'd just grin, he'd call on that charm, that seductive charm (that she had succumbed to all those years), he'd try to use it on them, but it wouldn't work, they wouldn't stop.

No, they would not stop. In their moving, they would follow her, they would refuse him, they would turn on him, they would scratch him, they would stomp on him, they would tear that charming smile right off his face.

"Go further!" she cried out. "Open it up, open yourselves up!" Two of the students began to falter. "Don't stop! Move more! Let out the sounds!"

Now.

They were running, they were jumping, they were leaping, they were shouting, and she in the midst of them, leading them, was as if possessed, propelled faster and faster, so fast that she was spun off from them into another orbit.

She found herself running, calling out to them, going further up the narrow path skirting the ravine. She tried to go fast, but the going had become hard, was getting harder. Something was on her back, holding her back, trying to force her to go this way, that way, any way but her own: An old woman was clinging to her, frail, wasting away, yet powerful, directing her.

She tried to evade her, she tried to change course, to throw her off, but she could not rid herself of this burden.

The women were following her, she could hear them calling out, she had to go on. They were the pursuer, she was being pursued, she was leading them, she was their mother, they were her children, she had been chosen, she had done the choosing, she was leading them to an ideal future, to the top, to the very top where she would be queen of a mountain not made of shit—

Stumbling she came to the edge of the cliff, to the very edge. It—her burden—the old woman—held tight, it would not let go.

She leaped, she cast herself out into space, she fell, pulling it—the old woman, the devil on her back—down, down, with her.

44

Now that I am old and almost still, I will soon be delivered.

First there will be forcing and going further, then there will be forcing and being stopped, then there will be forcing and going further again. There will be tightening and letting go, tightening and letting go, with smaller and smaller intervals between.

Now—soon—must come that exact moment when forcing becomes being forced, pushing becomes being pushed, thrusting becomes being thrust, out becomes in, closed becomes open, crying out becomes being cried out.

45

This country is not flat. It has rolling hills with here and there a small tree, shadowless in the searing overhead sun. In the concavity between three adjacent hills is an enormous amphitheater, the seats of stone and grass, the stage an open platform shielded by a makeshift curtain.

I make my way laboriously down the steep steps to the front of the amphitheater. I sit in the first row. I am the only one in the audience. Waiting, I sit and think of blood.

(Once a woman told me a story of death and the theater: With a companion some years ago she was traveling in a desert country. Driving a new car, they were objects of curiosity and jealousy to the native population. They stopped at a hotel in a small town for the night. The service and food were poor but they considered that this was part of their adventure. In the morning when they got up to go on, they discovered that there had been a double killing in the hotel. Two travelers in the room next door had been brutally murdered in their beds.

To their horror, the woman and her companion were accused of the crime. Nothing they said could convince the hotelkeeper of their innocence. They were hauled before the authorities and questioned in a language they barely understood. They kept asking to see an American consul, but of course there was no American consul nearby.

They were bound and put in separate cells. After several hours they were taken by a guard to a room empty except for two chairs facing a white curtain, improvised out of sheets. The overhead lights were turned off, the curtain was pulled back and a spotlight came on, shining upon the improvised stage. Before them was the scene of the crime, the hotel room, an exact duplicate of the room of the murder. And, in each bed, sitting up, were two huge puppets with faces and hair covered with blood. The police waited for the woman and her companion to cry out or in some way to indicate their guilt. But they did not cry out, they were too transfixed with terror.

Shortly afterward, they were released. An itinerant peddler had confessed to the crime. The woman suspected, though she could not be sure, that the peddler had already confessed when they were brought into the room with the puppets, but that the trial—the performance—, having been prepared, had to go on.)

The makeshift curtain is drawn back. A woman stands upon the stage. She raises her right arm slowly, raises her head, looks at the sky, lowers her arm, lowers her head. Now she is leaping. In one leap she covers almost the entire expanse of the stage. She turns and leaps in the other direction. She repeats the leaps, again and again. I am close enough to see the sweat on her face, on the skin of her bare arms. I can hear her breathing as she forces herself to go higher and higher. I can see the blood suffuse her face.

(Blood is not what it once was. Now one could not collect leftover blood, put it in a jar, store it in the refrigerator, pour it around plants as a fertilizer. Nor is my blood what it once was. Once the monthly spilling of my blood rooted me in the world's time, but that tie is long since cut. Now in multiple time I see—and am seen—with multiple eyes, the eyes of an old woman, a young woman, a woman of all the ages in between. As if I were an insect with swarms of eyes, looking forward, backward, to the side, up, down. Eyes having seen never stop seeing. Bones, nerves, muscles, fascia, tissue, tendons, blood, once having felt, never stop feeling.

Clearly blood inside story and blood outside story are not the same: They are not equivalent, they are not of the same type. They do not have the same electrophoresis patterns, the same antibodies, the same capacity to clot. Blood outside story can be isolated, can be cooked, scalded, mixed with agar, an extract of seaweed, for examination. Blood inside story cannot be separated out.)

Three young women in white appear on stage. They arrange themselves in a line, heads bent and arms at their sides. They look furtively at each other. First one, then the other, then the third, not quite in unison, slowly begin to raise their arms, palms out. They hold them there, head turned up, eyes staring at the sky, then slowly lower them. They begin to lean from the waist, arms crossed over their breasts, leaning first to one side, then to the other, in a slow rocking motion. One draws apart, turns and falls to the ground. The two others circle about her, holding their arms out to her in an imploring gesture, but she lies inert. The two standing join together. Arms linked, heads turned to the side and down, they lean, they rock. Now one of them moves apart, turn and slowly falls to the ground, next to the one lying there. The third, remaining upright, circles the two on the ground, imploring, leaning, rocking, imploring.

(Once in a strange country, in an old city, I came upon

179

an old graveyard, between stone walls. The dirt upon which the graves stood was mounded. Here a grave was thrust up, there another one, in the crowded space. For so many years had the burying gone on in that little graveyard that the dead had been buried on top of the dead, layered one upon the other, unevenly, till now it seemed the ones underneath were straining to push the new ones off.)

The three young women reappear, dressed in black. Once again they arrange themselves in a line, heads bent and arms at their sides. They begin to twist from side to side, faster and faster, in a sharp jerking movement. They are not in unison. I see the stain of sweat spreading on their black clothes, making the black blacker. The jerky spasms move from one to the other—to me—like fire.

Once again the leaping woman leaps, in one direction, and then in the other. Once again the three young women appear, this time dressed in ordinary clothes. They do stylized motions of cleaning, of washing, of sweeping, of dusting, of sewing. Sewing, they are themselves the needles, piercing through the cloth of the air.

(Now I remember how the air, the sun, the sky was in Peralta. I remember how every morning the fog lay over the valley, how every noon, the fog burned off and the sun appeared in a high widening sky, how every evening the fog gathered once again, mounded over the western hills like an incoming tide, ready to cover and protect the valley during the night. The daily cycle suggested, the soft air itself suggested—we wanted, we needed it to suggest—that what had been done could be undone. There had been so much death, so many huge deaths in the just past, uncountable, incomprehensible, not to be thought of.)

I turn and see several other women are dispersed within the amphitheater. One is weeping.

The stage is now crowded with women. In place, they begin to turn. They go faster and faster till they are whirling like dervishes, round and round again. Clinging to the back of each woman is an old woman, frail, almost transparent in her frailty, driving the dancer on to further turning.

(Look at me, look at how high I can still kick, my mother once said to me, her leg swinging up from her hip clumsily. She was standing by my kitchen counter. She was not as old as I am now.)

Now each time the women turn, at the end of each revolution, they kick clumsily, from the hip. The audience—for there is a large audience—begins to laugh. I too begin to laugh. I make myself laugh. I cannot stop. The audience has turned and is watching me. I try to stop laughing but now I am howling (with rage, with shame). I feel myself ludicrous, stupid, ugly, a gargoyle, everyone else's terror in the glass. I feel my legs turn in, my hands clutch, my abdomen contract, my spine curve. I am crouching lower and lower, being forced down through a hole in myself, a gutter red and dark to a single point between motion and stillness, between the going that I am coming from and the coming I am going towards.

About the Author

Millicent Dillon is a biographer, a novelist, a short story writer and a playwright. Her biographies include *A Little Original Sin: The Life and Work of Jane Bowles,* and *After Egypt: Isadora Duncan and Mary Cassatt.* Her fiction includes *Baby Perpetua and Other Stories,* and the novel *The One In the Back Is Medea.* Her plays include *She Is In Tangier* (based on *A Little Original Sin*), and *Prisoners of Ordinary Need* which was part of the San Francisco Playwrights Festival 1990. A native New Yorker, she has lived for many years in San Francisco.